Rescuing Macie

Also from Susan Stoker

Claiming Felicity
Claiming Sarah (Sept 2019)

Mountain Mercenaries Series:
Defending Allye
Defending Chloe
Defending Morgan
Defending Harlow (June 2019)
Defending Everly (Dec 2019)
Defending Zara (Mar 2020)
Defending Raven (July 2020)

SEAL of Protection: Legacy Series:
Securing Caite
Securing Sidney (May 2019)
Securing Piper (Sept 2019)
Securing Zoey (Jan 2020)
Securing Avery (TBA)
Securing Kalee (TBA)

SEAL of Protection Series:
Protecting Caroline
Protecting Alabama
Protecting Alabama's Kids
Protecting Fiona
Marrying Caroline (novella)
Protecting Summer
Protecting Cheyenne
Protecting Jessyka
Protecting Julie (novella)
Protecting Melody
Protecting the Future
Protecting Alabama's Kids (novella)
Protecting Kiera (novella)
Protecting Dakota

Stand-Alone:
The Guardian Mist

Nature's Rift
A Princess for Cale
A Moment in Time
Lambert's Lady

Beyond Reality Series:
Outback Hearts
Flaming Hearts
Frozen Hearts

Writing as Annie George:
Stepbrother Virgin (erotic novella)

Rescuing Macie

By Susan Stoker

A Delta Force Heroes Novella

1001 Dark Nights

EVIL EYE
CONCEPTS

Rescuing Macie
A Delta Force Heroes Novella
Copyright 2019 Susan Stoker
ISBN: 978-1-948050-82-1

Published by Evil Eye Concepts, Incorporated

Author's Note

The first time I saw a 1001 Dark Nights book, I wasn't sure what it was about. But after reading a few of the stories, I was hooked. It had been a dream of mine to be invited to write in the series and when Liz Berry did ask if I was interested, it took me about two point one seconds to say, "Yes!"

This wasn't a book that was supposed to happen. I had planned on ending the Delta Force Heroes series with Mary and Truck's book. But after being invited to write in the 1001 Dark Nights world, I had to think of whose story I should write.

Deciding to give Truck a sister who suffers from anxiety feels like a right choice. I asked my readers who have anxiety to try to explain some of what they go through when they're having an attack. I used a lot of what they told me. I know I probably made some mistakes, but I tried to keep to the facts and show what people who have anxiety suffer from on a daily basis.

This book is for all my Delta Force Heroes fans who didn't want to see the series end.

It's for anyone who ever has experienced an anxiety attack and felt like less of a person as a result. You deserve love just like everyone else and if you haven't found it yet, please don't give up.

And lastly, this is for Liz. Thank you for inviting me to be a part of your family. For your advice and encouragement and for being so wonderful.

Sign up for the 1001 Dark Nights Newsletter
and be entered to win a Tiffany Key necklace.

There's a contest every month!

Go to www.1001DarkNights.com to subscribe.

As a bonus, all subscribers can download
FIVE FREE exclusive books!

One Thousand and One Dark Nights

Once upon a time, in the future…

*I was a student fascinated with stories and learning.
I studied philosophy, poetry, history, the occult, and
the art and science of love and magic. I had a vast
library at my father's home and collected thousands
of volumes of fantastic tales.*

*I learned all about ancient races and bygone
times. About myths and legends and dreams of all
people through the millennium. And the more I read
the stronger my imagination grew until I discovered
that I was able to travel into the stories… to actually
become part of them.*

*I wish I could say that I listened to my teacher
and respected my gift, as I ought to have. If I had, I
would not be telling you this tale now.
But I was foolhardy and confused, showing off
with bravery.*

*One afternoon, curious about the myth of the
Arabian Nights, I traveled back to ancient Persia to
see for myself if it was true that every day Shahryar
(Persian: شهريار, "king") married a new virgin, and then
sent yesterday's wife to be beheaded. It was written
and I had read, that by the time he met Scheherazade,
the vizier's daughter, he'd killed one thousand
women.*

Something went wrong with my efforts. I arrived in the midst of the story and somehow exchanged places with Scheherazade – a phenomena that had never occurred before and that still to this day, I cannot explain.

Now I am trapped in that ancient past. I have taken on Scheherazade's life and the only way I can protect myself and stay alive is to do what she did to protect herself and stay alive.

Every night the King calls for me and listens as I spin tales. And when the evening ends and dawn breaks, I stop at a point that leaves him breathless and yearning for more. And so the King spares my life for one more day, so that he might hear the rest of my dark tale.

As soon as I finish a story... I begin a new one... like the one that you, dear reader, have before you now.

Chapter One

Mercedes Laughlin was in bed reading when she heard the noise.

At first she didn't think much about it. She heard random noises at night all the time. The apartment building she lived in wasn't exactly quiet. There were people coming and going at all hours of the day and night, and she'd definitely heard her share of domestic arguments.

Macie's apartment was on the second floor and toward the back of the building. She loved how she could see a creek meandering through acres of trees from her living room. And since she spent most of her time there, sitting at her desk and working on her computer, it was soothing. It wasn't the most expensive apartment complex in Lampasas, but it wasn't a shit hole either. All in all, she'd lucked out in finding a place where she felt safe and could be near her brother.

But the noise she'd heard was unusual. It wasn't like the sounds she heard from outside…cars driving by, people talking, it sounded as if it was right inside her apartment.

Putting her ereader aside, she held her breath and waited to see if she'd hear the odd sound again.

When she did—and it sounded closer—Macie froze. Then she heard a voice.

"Shut up, you idiot! We don't want her to wake up until we're in her room."

"She's not going to hear me shuffling across the floor, but she *is* going to hear your dumb ass talking. So *you* shut the fuck up!"

Without thought, Macie threw back her covers, grabbed her cell phone, and headed for her closet and the sort-of safe room she had there. But the next words from whoever was in her apartment made her stop in her tracks.

"Remember, if she's not in bed when we get there, check the back of the closet. He said that's where the shit'll be and where she'll probably hide anyway. If we push on the right side, the door'll open up."

"You gonna let me have first crack at her?"

Macie was breathing hard now, and she felt dizzy, but she didn't hesitate as she changed course and headed for the window instead.

As someone who suffered from anxiety, she'd made sure she had a place to feel completely safe inside her apartment. She'd hired a local carpenter to build a false wall in the back of the walk-in closet. There was just enough space behind it that she could sit and be comfortable. She used the space when she needed absolute darkness and quiet, or when she was simply overwhelmed with whatever was going on in her life.

But that hidey-hole wouldn't keep her safe tonight. Whoever the men were in her apartment, they knew about it, and it was obviously the first place they'd look for her.

She definitely didn't like the sound of the one man wanting "first crack" at her.

So she was resorting to Plan B.

Her first choice would always be to hide inside. Away from the world. Cocooned from prying eyes and judgmental stares. But being pragmatic, she also knew if a tornado came through, or if there was a fire, she couldn't hide inside the apartment. She needed an escape route. And that was the other reason why she'd chosen this unit.

Right outside her bedroom was a large tree. It wasn't easy, but she could jump from the window ledge onto the large branch that grew perpendicular to the ground, toward the building. She knew she could do it because she'd practiced. Always in the middle of the night, when no one was around to see what she was doing and judge her.

Every moment of her life, Macie worried about what people thought of her. Were they looking at her and laughing about her clothes? Did her hair look weird? After she met someone, she always wondered if she'd said the right things, if they were talking about her to their friends.

It was a curse, and she hated feeling the way she did, but she couldn't turn it off. She took Lexapro daily to try to control her anxiety and to quiet the voices in her head that were constantly telling her she wasn't good enough, smart enough, or capable of doing her job. And when needed, she took a Vistaril tablet, which made her feel nothing at all, and that was bliss when her anxiety got the better of her.

Knowing her apartment wasn't that big and she had mere seconds before the men came into her room, Macie quickly raised the window, thankful that she'd recently made sure it was in good working order, and eyed the tree branch. Her breaths came out in short puffs and she could feel the tips of her fingers begin to tingle. She really wanted to run back in and grab her meds, but she had no time.

"Remember, he's not sure if she's already found the stuff, but if we get it tonight, we'll earn an extra grand. So don't spend too much time with the bitch."

"Awwww, come on. I love it when they cry and fight. It makes it that much better."

There was a muffled smacking sound and a quiet *umph* before the first man said, "We get the shit first. Then if there's time, you can have your fun."

The men were whispering, but she could still hear them clearly. Macie didn't have to be a rocket scientist to know what they were talking about. At least when it came to the "fun" the one man wanted. She had no clue what they could possibly be looking for, but she'd run out of time to even think about it.

If she'd been asleep, she wouldn't have heard them until it was too late.

Shoving her cell phone in the waistband of the sleep shorts she had on, Macie ducked and climbed onto the windowsill. It was second nature to make sure she always had her phone on her. She needed the security it provided. The small electronic device was a way to get help if her anxiety completely overwhelmed her…which it had more than once.

She wished that she could find a way to close the window after she jumped, so the men in her bedroom wouldn't know where she'd gone, but it was too late to think of that now.

Hyperventilating, Macie eyed the branch—and jumped.

She let out an *umph* when she landed on her stomach on the limb. She held on for dear life, but felt extremely shaky and wasn't sure she could hang on. She vaguely felt her inner thighs burning from scraping along the rough bark, but the pain barely registered. She had probably thirty seconds or so, tops, before one of the men looked out the window. They'd probably see the empty bed and go straight to the closet first. At least she hoped that's what they would do. It would buy her a bit of time.

Scrambling to her feet quickly and carefully, Macie shuffled along the large branch, holding on to the smaller limbs above her as she made her way toward the trunk. She began to climb downward as fast as she could, mentally counting the seconds. When she'd practiced this, she'd always been wearing jeans and sneakers. Bare feet and pajama shorts weren't exactly conducive to a middle-of-the-night escape.

Macie was trying to be quiet while still moving as fast as possible. Climbing down was harder because of her lack of proper clothing and the way her entire body was shaking. Stretching her leg down to the final branch, she sighed in relief, thinking she'd made it.

"Hey!" a low voice shouted from above her.

She startled so bad, she missed the branch and tumbled the three feet or so to the ground, landing on her ass. Without looking up at her window, Macie leaped to her feet and took off running. As she ran, she pulled out her cell phone—which had miraculously not fallen out of her shorts as she'd climbed out of the tree—and frantically pushed one of the saved numbers as she tried to figure out where she could hide.

* * * *

Colonel Colton Robinson ran a hand over his face wearily. It was oh-two-thirty in the morning and both Delta Force teams were finishing up their debrief of the mission they'd just returned from. The fourteen men, from two different teams, had worked together to bring down a high-value target who had been hiding out in Africa. Logistically, the last week and a half had been a bitch, but Colt had never doubted the men under his command for a second.

Ghost's team was older and more experienced, and tended to err on the side of caution. All seven men were married, some had children, so their main concern was getting home to their families safe and sound. Trigger's team, on the other hand, was younger, mostly late twenties and early thirties, and all of them single. They had no problem taking risks and doing everything necessary to get the job done.

Together, the fourteen men were the best he'd ever had the pleasure to command. Colt trusted each and every one of them, and the latest mission had been no exception. The HVT was neutralized and they'd done it without blowing their cover. As far as the African government and the terrorist organization was concerned, the man had died in a local skirmish, not at the hands of the US military.

Colt knew everyone was anxious to get home, but debriefing was required. He listened as Lefty explained how they'd exited the compound where the HVT had been holed up. Colt knew all the details, but protocol demanded they review it one more time.

He heard the unmistakable sound of a phone vibrating and turned to frown at the man sitting to his left. Truck knew they weren't supposed to have their phones on, but at least he'd had the decency to put it on vibrate. Colt wouldn't reprimand him—if *he* had a wife or kids at home, he'd want them to be able to get ahold of him at any time—but he glared at Truck to let him know that he was walking a fine line.

Truck looked down at his phone and frowned. He brought the phone to his ear. "Mace? What are—"

The second Truck said his sister's name, Colt straightened in his chair and all his attention was on the soldier sitting next to him.

So many times in the last two months, he'd wanted to ask Truck for his sister's number, but he didn't want to pressure Macie with his attention if she didn't want it. And he had to assume she didn't, because he'd flat-out asked her if he could see her again the last time they'd been together—and she'd snuck out of his house without a word or leaving him a way to contact her.

The memories of the last time he'd seen Macie were interrupted when Truck stood and moved toward the door, the phone still to his ear.

Without thought, Colt stood and followed Truck. At the last second, he turned to the group of men still sitting around the table. "Dismissed," he said absently. They'd finish the debrief later.

"Sir?" Ghost called as Colt was about to disappear.

He waved at the man and said, "I'll call if we need you." And then he was rushing after Truck down the hallway.

"Mace, slow down. What's wrong?" Truck asked.

Colt's blood ran cold. He hurried to catch up, trying to control himself and not rip the phone out of Truck's hand.

"I'm coming!" he said urgently. "Find a place to hide. I'm on my way."

That was it. Colt was done. "Give me the phone," he ordered.

Truck's gaze went to his, and his brows drew down in surprise and annoyance.

Colt wiggled his fingers. "Give her to me. You drive. I'll talk."

Surprisingly, Truck nodded and handed him his phone. Both men ran down the hall to the door that led out to the parking lot. Colt reached in his pocket and threw his keychain at Truck even as he brought the phone up to his ear. "Macie?"

"Yeah?" was the weak answer.

"It's Colt. From Truck's wedding. What's going on? Where are you?" He could hear her wheezing as she hyperventilated, and it only increased his concern.

"My apartment. Men broke in. I got out but I don't know where to go!"

Colt's heart dropped at her words. He and Truck arrived at his Jeep Wrangler and both jumped in. He pulled out his own cell and dialed 9-1-1, then handed it to Truck. The other man started the Jeep and began talking to the dispatcher at the same time. Within seconds, they were racing out of the parking lot and headed for the front gate of the Army post.

"What do you see around you?" Colt asked Macie. "Look around, Macie. Tell me what you're looking at," he ordered.

"A big open parking area. Trees at the edge."

"Are there lights? Cars parked close together?"

"Lights near the buildings, not as many farther out. There's lots of cars. Oh shit…" she said.

"What? Macie, talk to me," Colt barked.

"I hear the men," Macie whispered. "They're looking for me."

The terror in her voice made panic rise within Colt and he held the phone against his chest for a second to try to regain his composure. He turned to Truck. "Hurry. Drive as fast as you fucking can. They're hunting her."

The second the words left his mouth, Colt felt the Jeep lurch forward. It was a good thing it was the middle of the night and no one was on the streets. Truck was driving like a bat out of hell.

It was thirty miles to Lampasas. There was no way they could get there in time to help if the assholes got their hands on her. Truck had called the cops, but Colt knew what he told Macie in the next couple minutes could be a matter of life and death.

"Head away from the lights. If it's dark, they can't see where you are exactly," he told her urgently. "Do you understand?"

"Y-yeah."

"Have they seen you?"

"I-I don't think so."

She was breathing hard and still wheezing. Colt's chest hurt for her. "Good. Head for a row of cars as far away from the lights as possible. Get under one. Not behind it, but under it. Then if you need to, you can crawl under the one next to it. Then the next. Keep moving if you have to. If it's possible, work your way around the cars until you get to a section of vehicles they've already checked. As a last resort, head into the trees, but *only* if they don't see you. The last thing you want is to go farther away from civilization where the men could do whatever they want to you without someone hearing or seeing. Understand?"

She didn't answer him, but he heard her breaths coming quick and shallow through the phone.

"I'm here," he said, forcing his voice to lower and calm. She needed him to be her rock right now. He couldn't let her hear one ounce of panic in his tone. "I've got you, Macie. You're doing great. Just listen to me. You're amazing. I'm sure they didn't expect you to outsmart them. Just keep doing what you're doing. You've got this." Colt kept up the litany of praise even as he gripped the phone so tightly his fingers were cramping.

He glanced at the speedometer and saw that Truck was doing ninety-five. The Wrangler shook slightly from the speed, but the only thing Colt could think was, *Go faster. God, just go faster.*

"They're coming this way," Macie said—and Colt lowered his chin to his chest, closed his eyes and prayed harder than he'd ever prayed before.

* * * *

Macie had no idea what Colt was doing with her brother at two-thirty in the morning, but she couldn't deny that she was extremely grateful. She didn't even flinch when Colt called her brother Truck. He'd apparently been given the nickname when he'd joined the Army. She was trying to remember to call him that, but because he'd been Ford to her as long as she could remember, it was tough.

And as much as she knew her brother would've helped her, hearing Colt's steady voice kept her grounded. She remembered after Truck's wedding, when she'd been having an anxiety attack, he'd held her against him and talked to her in his low, rumbly voice. How much it had helped. He'd calmed her and helped pull her out of the dark place her mind had gone.

The same was happening tonight. She'd been panicking and running headlong through the parking lot, with no idea what to do or where to go, when he'd forced her to pay attention to her surroundings. He gave her something to concentrate on, and it felt good to let him take over and tell her what to do.

She had no idea why he hadn't called her after her brother's wedding. He'd asked her out and she'd badly wanted to spend more time with him, but he hadn't called. Hadn't gotten in touch with her. His rejection had hurt, but she really wasn't surprised. She was a pain in the ass and no one as amazing as Colt would want to be with her.

At the moment, however, she had more pressing issues to think about. Looking back toward the building, Macie didn't see any sign of the men who'd broken into her apartment, but she could hear their footsteps. Macie ducked behind a car and dropped to her knees.

She winced but ignored the pain and crawled between a row of cars, making sure to stay out of sight. Then she lay down on her belly and crawled under one of the cars in the lot. She was wearing a tight tank top and her sleep shorts, because she hated to feel constricted by clothing when she slept.

"Macie?" Colt asked.

She opened her mouth to respond when she heard one of the men saying to his friend, "She has to be this way. We've checked all the other cars."

It felt like she was having a heart attack. Her chest was tight and she couldn't get enough air into her lungs. But she couldn't gasp for oxygen because they'd hear her.

Macie mentally berated herself for calling her brother and not the police. If she'd called 9-1-1, they'd probably be here by now.

"Easy, Mace," Colt said in her ear. She ground her teeth together and forced herself to listen to him rather than the two men who were still looking for her. "You can do this. You told me that you used to play Army with Truck when you were younger. This is the same thing.

Remember when you hid in that bush one afternoon and he couldn't find you anywhere? See if you can do that again. It's dark where you are, right? If you're quiet, they'll never see you. They'll walk right on by."

Macie nodded, even though Colt couldn't see her. She'd told him about hiding from her big brother when she was at Colt's house, the night of Ford's wedding. She'd crawled under a bush next to a neighbor's house and her brother hadn't been able to find her. Eventually she'd fallen asleep, and Ford had been beside himself with worry, thinking that she'd been snatched off the street. He'd walked by her hiding place dozens of times without knowing she was there.

It was only a matter of time before one of the men found her under the car, though. This wasn't a game, and she wasn't a kid anymore. Macie was sure they were looking under each and every one of the vehicles. It wouldn't work to simply roll under the one next to her; eventually she'd run out of cars and be stuck.

Quickly, still trying to be as quiet as she could, Macie backed up. Her knees were getting torn to pieces, but she barely felt the rough asphalt digging into them. She wiggled her way to the back side of the SUV she was huddled under and turned around. She was at the edge of the parking lot, and there was a row of hedges, then the trees and creek she so loved to look at while she was working.

Remembering what Colt had said, she resisted the urge to get up and run into the trees. Instead, she stayed on her hands and knees and hurriedly crawled to the thick hedge. She pushed her way between the leaves, thankful it wasn't winter and there were actually leaves to hide behind. The branches scratched at her arms, but again, she didn't feel the slight sting. At five-seven, she wasn't exactly small, but she brought her knees up to her chest and wrapped an arm around them. She brought the phone to her ear and ducked her head into her knees, trying to make herself as small as possible.

"I crawled into a bunch of bushes," she said in a toneless whisper. "Colt?"

"Yeah, Mace? I'm here. Are you hidden? Are you safe? Are the men still looking for you?"

"I can't breathe."

"Yes you can. You're doing amazing. In and out. Remember how you breathed with me that night? Close your eyes. Imagine we're back in my bed. I'm behind you, and my hand is on your chest. In…and out.

Slow down your breaths, Mace. That's it. They're gonna walk right by you. They can't see you. In…and out. That's good. You're doing great."

Amazingly, his voice in her ear, along with the way she was pinching her thigh to try to force her attention away from her situation, was working. She breathed with him, not making a sound. Macie could feel her lungs loosening up a bit.

"You start on that side, I'll start over here. If she's not under the cars, I'm guessing she ran into the trees. We can catch up with her and make sure she hasn't found the shit and blabbed about it to the pigs."

"Then I can have my fun?" the other man asked.

"Jesus, you have a one-track mind. Yes, once she spills her guts, you can do whatever the fuck you want with her."

Their voices were loud enough that Colt heard them.

"Don't listen to them, Mace. Concentrate only on me. You're good. We're almost there. You just have to hang on for another couple minutes. You can do that. Piece of cake."

Colt's voice was almost as good as the drugs she used to control her anxiety and panic attacks. Almost.

Macie heard the men getting closer and closer to her hiding spot, and she felt her breathing speed up once more. She couldn't help it. They were going to find her and torture her until she gave them information. She had no idea what they were looking for when they'd broken in, but she'd tell them whatever they wanted as long as they didn't hurt her.

"Eaaaaasy, honey. You've got this."

That was the thing. She *didn't* have this. But by some miracle, Colt thought she did. His voice was still even and controlled.

"Shit. She's not here!" one of the men complained after they'd passed by her hiding spot.

"Come on, she's got to be here somewhere. She's barefoot and in her fucking pajamas. No cars have left, so she hasn't driven off. Stupid bitch is just hiding from us. You go that way and I'll—"

His voice abruptly cut off when the sound of sirens wailed in the distance.

"Fuck. She called the fucking cops!" the man who wanted to "have his way with her" said. "We gotta get out of here."

"Dammit. There goes that extra thousand," the other man complained. "We'll come back after the cops leave. She won't get away again."

Macie didn't move a muscle after she heard the men run off. She stayed where she was, refusing to do something stupid, like come out of her hiding place too soon and have the men catch her after everything she'd done to keep away from them.

"Are those sirens?" Colt asked in her ear.

Macie nodded, knowing he couldn't see her, but not able to speak. Her vocal cords had closed up and refused to work. Her lips were dry and she didn't have enough spit in her mouth to even lick them.

"Don't come out, hon. Just stay where you are. We'll be there in"– there was a pause and Macie could imagine him looking over at her brother—"less than ten minutes. Even if you hear the cops, just stay put. Truck'll tell the 9-1-1 operator that you're too scared to come out. You won't get in trouble. Hear me?"

Macie nodded again, but didn't speak.

"I'm proud of you, Mace. You're doing great. You did the right thing. You got out of your apartment, called for help, and stayed hidden. That's exactly what you should've done."

His praise was like a balm to her soul. She wasn't sure she believed him—she felt like the biggest coward ever—but for now, right this second, she chose to take his words to heart.

She could hear the sirens getting louder and louder, but she kept her concentration on Colt. If she didn't, she knew she'd completely fall apart.

* * * *

Colt ignored the looks Truck was shooting him from the driver's seat. He knew the other man was going to have a lot to say to him later...not that he could blame him. He was just getting to know his sister again, and obviously hadn't known about the fact she suffered from anxiety— or that his commander had spent the night with her after Truck's wedding.

They hadn't *done* anything, but Colt didn't think that was going to matter to Truck.

His entire focus right now was on Macie. He could hear her breathing on the other end of the line and could hear the sirens wailing in the background, but most importantly, he no longer heard the men who were searching for her.

He continued his litany of soothing words, not wanting her to move until he could get to her, holding on to the handle over his head as Truck continued to drive like a man possessed. Truck wasn't fucking around. He'd pushed the Wrangler as far as it could be pushed. It was a miracle they hadn't been stopped by a cop. Even with his credentials and the fact that Truck was on the phone with an emergency operator, he didn't think a police officer would be amused at how recklessly Truck was driving.

Truck clicked off the phone and Colt looked over at him. The other man's lips were pressed tightly together, and he looked like he was about two seconds from losing his shit. Colt wanted to tell Truck to pull himself together, that the last thing his sister needed to see was him freaking out, but he couldn't, because he was still talking to Macie.

"Macie? We're almost there. I can see your apartment complex ahead. It's lit up like a Christmas tree with all the blue and red lights from the police who are there. You're safe. We're here. Stay put until I come and get you though, okay?"

She hadn't been answering him, but for that question, he got a slight murmur. Even that made him feel better.

He didn't know exactly where she was, but once Truck pulled into the lot, he looked around and tried to see it from Macie's perspective. "Where's her apartment?" he asked Truck. The other man pointed toward a building to the left.

Nodding, Colt climbed out of the Jeep and headed in that direction. He was stopped by Truck's hand on his arm. "You get my sister and I'll speak to the cops. But we need to talk. *Sir*."

The rank was tacked on at the end of his sentence in such a way that it more than communicated Truck's irritation with his commanding officer.

Nodding at him, Colt turned to head toward a row of cars on the back side of the parking lot. There weren't lights covering the entire blacktop and he could see dark shapes in the distance that he imagined were the trees Macie had described to him.

He remembered her talking about how beautiful they were and how she liked to look at them when she was working at her desk in her apartment. She'd recovered from her anxiety attack after the wedding reception and had been relaxed and warm in his arms. Right afterward,

Colt had told her that he wanted to take her to dinner, and she hadn't agreed or disagreed. He'd taken that as a good sign, but of course he'd been wrong, as she'd left the next morning without a word and without waking him up.

Shaking off his memories, Colt concentrated on finding Macie. "I'm here," he told her quietly through the phone. "You're going to need to come out so I can get to you. If those other men couldn't find you, there's not a chance in hell that I will." He was lying, but he wanted to reassure her that her hiding place was secure. That she'd done a good job.

"Mace? You can come out now. Your brother is here. You're safe."

He waited a heartbeat…then he heard rustling coming from his left. He turned toward the row of hedges that looked way too skimpy to have concealed a full-grown woman, but sure enough, Macie was crawling out of the bushes.

Clicking off Truck's phone, he shoved it into his back pocket even as he jogged toward Macie. She was on her hands and knees, and she looked up at him with wide eyes.

Without thought, he dropped to his knees and took her into his arms. Instead of recoiling, she latched on to him so tightly, he couldn't tell where she ended and he began. He could feel her heart beating way too damn fast against his chest, and she buried her face into the space between his neck and shoulder. Her arms wrapped around him and she clutched at his back. It felt as if she were literally trying to crawl inside him.

"Shhhh," he murmured. "I've got you. You're safe."

Macie didn't cry. She simply held on to him as if he was the only thing between her and certain death. And in a way, he supposed he maybe had been.

How long they stayed like that, he couldn't say. All he knew was how good she felt in his arms and how fucking relieved he was that she was okay. Finally, Colt forced himself to loosen his hold and draw back from her. She resisted, but he reached up and took her wrists in his hands. Her pulse was still hammering as if she'd run a mile.

"Hi, Mace," he said with a smile.

She did her best to return his smile, but it quickly faded from her face.

"Are you hurt?"

"No. At least I don't think so," she said softly.

Colt looked her over as best he could, but as it was dark in this corner of the parking area, he couldn't see much. She was wearing a dark-colored tank top and shorts that matched. He absently had the thought that he was glad she hadn't been wearing white before he eased to his feet, pulling her with him.

"Oh!" she exclaimed when she was standing and her knees suddenly buckled.

Colt didn't waste time asking what was wrong. He simply put an arm behind her back and one under her knees and picked her up.

She grabbed at him. "Don't drop me!"

"Of course not. You don't weigh any more than the packs I used to carry on missions," Colt reassured her. "I've got you." He saw that she still clutched her cell phone in her hand and didn't bother telling her to put it away. First, he had no idea where she'd put it, but second, it had been her lifeline, and he'd let her hold on to it for as long as she needed if it made her feel more secure.

He started walking toward the spinning lights of the cop cars, where they'd no doubt find Truck.

She rested her head on his shoulder, and Colt felt as if he were ten feet tall. He loved the way Macie fit in his arms, how she felt. He didn't care about her anxiety. Nobody was perfect. And if he could make her feel better about herself and about things going on in her life, he'd be satisfied.

Chapter Two

Macie sat sideways in a chair at her dining room table and watched with wary eyes as the police and detectives wandered through her apartment. Truck was standing off to her left with his arms crossed over his chest and a scowl on his face. After draping a blanket around her shoulders, Colt sat in front of her, holding her hand. In fact, he hadn't let go of it since he'd carried her away from her hiding spot.

"Why don't you tell me everything that happened tonight," the detective sitting across from her said in a no-nonsense tone.

"She needs to take her medicine first," Colt insisted, then turned to Macie. "Are your pills in your bathroom?"

She nodded. "I can go and get them," she told him quietly.

"I got it. What am I looking for?" Truck asked.

Macie looked down at her lap. This wasn't the way she'd wanted Truck to find out how messed-up she was. He was strong and brave and amazing, and the last thing he'd want to deal with was a sister who was crazy. He'd—

"Macie," Colt said firmly, making her raise her head to look at him. "Where are your pills?"

"In the cabinet to the left of the sinks. I need one of the Vistaril tablets," she told him.

"Be right back," Truck said.

"I know this is hard, but you're doing great," Colt said. "Just hang on a little longer and we'll get you to a quiet place where you can relax, okay?"

Macie nodded. She had no idea where that would be, but she knew Colt wanted her to agree, so she did. Her head was pounding and she felt shaky from her anxiety attack. And the worst thing was that her nightmare wasn't over. She was going to have to talk about what happened and what she'd heard. Then her brother, Colt, and the cops would leave, and she'd be alone again, and the men said that they'd be back and—

This time Colt simply threaded his fingers with hers and held on tightly. He always seemed to know when she was lost in her head, when she was over-worrying.

Truck was back within seconds, holding a small pill in his hand. He handed her a cup full of water and she swallowed the pill gratefully. If there ever was a time when she needed to be numb, it was now.

"Take your time," Colt said gently. "When you're ready, walk us through what happened tonight."

Wanting to get it over with, Macie didn't hesitate. "I couldn't sleep so I was reading. I heard a weird noise, and then heard two men talking. They were being quiet, and if I had been asleep I wouldn't have heard them, but because I was up, I did." She knew she wasn't being very articulate, but no one interrupted her, which she was grateful for.

"What were they saying?" the detective asked.

Macie's hand tightened on Colt's involuntarily. She didn't want to repeat what they'd said. What if Colt decided she was somehow to blame for what had happened tonight? What if Ford decided she was too much trouble and wouldn't want to keep talking to her?

"Breathe," Colt said softly. "You're safe. Your brother and I won't let anything happen to you."

She looked up at him and saw the sincerity in his eyes. She had no idea what a man like Colt was doing here with her. She was fucked up. *Seriously* fucked up. But she was also weak enough to not give a damn right now. She needed him.

"At first, they were arguing about whether or not I could hear them. They knew about my safe room. They were going to see if I was in bed, and if not, the first place they were going to look was my room in my closet."

"You have a safe room?" the detective asked, sitting up straighter in his chair.

"Sort of. It's not *really* a safe room. It's just a place I like to go when I need complete darkness. I get migraines, and it helps to be somewhere with no light," Macie explained. She could've gone on and told the police officer about how sometimes it was the only place she felt safe, how she liked to hide there when her anxiety overwhelmed her, but, ever aware of how people perceived her, she kept her mouth shut.

"How big is it?" the detective asked.

"Not big at all. Maybe around six feet long by three feet wide. I just had a false wall put in the back of my closet," she explained.

"Okay. Go on. What happened next?"

Macie took a breath and continued. "The men were there to pick something up. They said if they got it tonight, they'd get a bonus from whoever hired them."

She glanced at her brother and saw him run a hand through his hair in agitation. Just seeing him so stressed out made her own anxiety level climb.

Macie used her free hand to pinch the skin at the top of thigh. Sometimes the slight pain helped keep her in the moment and not completely freak out. "Yeah. They said they were there to pick something up."

"What were they looking for?" the detective broke in.

Macie knew this question was coming. She'd been trying to think of what in the world someone could want of hers, but had come up blank. Knowing it was important the officer believed her, she raised her head and looked him in the eyes. "I don't know. I don't know who the men were who broke in. I don't know what they were looking for. I don't know how they knew about my safe room. I don't know why they'd be interested in someone like me. I'm nobody. I don't meet a lot of people. I work from home. Most days, the only people I talk to are online. I don't understand *any* of this."

She felt Colt squeeze her hand. Then she felt him nudge her other hand off her thigh and rub the spot she'd pinched. It was almost uncanny how much he *saw* her. It made her uncomfortable, but at the same time it felt good.

"How'd you get out?" Colt asked.

She turned her gaze on him. She liked looking at his warm, compassionate eyes more than looking at the hardened face of the detective. She could tell the cop didn't believe her. That he thought she was hiding something. If she knew what the men were after, she'd give it to them, no questions asked. The last thing she wanted was someone hunting her.

"I jumped out my window," she said matter-of-factly.

"Jesus Christ," Truck swore.

Macie flinched at the harsh words from her brother.

"More, Macie. Give us more," Colt said firmly.

She took a deep breath and kept her eyes on Colt. "You know I need to have an escape route. I did it at your house, too."

He nodded. "The first thing you did was look out the windows, test to be sure you could open the one in my bedroom, and scope out how you could get out of the house."

"Right. Because if there was a fire or an earthquake, I needed to know where to go. What to do."

"Makes sense. Go on," Colt urged.

"There's a big tree right outside my window. I picked this apartment because of it. It's close enough to my bedroom, and has branches big enough that if I needed to, I could jump out of my window and get down."

"Is that how you got these?" Colt asked, running his fingers lightly over the scrapes on her legs and arms.

Macie shrugged. "Some. The ones on my knees I got from crawling in the parking lot."

"Mace," Truck said, then he was kneeling in front of her. "God, I'm so sorry. But...you also have to know, I'm so fucking proud of you."

She blinked. Proud of her? He was *proud* of her?

"I was a coward," she told him. "I was so scared. I didn't even call the cops. Those guys would've gotten me if it wasn't for you and Colt."

Truck brought a hand up to her head and brushed her hair back from her face. "You are *not* a coward," he scolded. "You did what had to be done. You got out of the situation. Believe me, that's the most important thing you could've done."

"Okay. So you jumped out your window and climbed down a tree. Then you hid, right? And the men came after you?" the detective asked, obviously wanting to move the interview along.

Truck gave her one last caress, then stood back up and leaned against the wall once more.

Macie cleared her throat. "Yeah. Colt told me to hide, so I got under a car in the far part of the parking lot. But the men figured out that's where I'd most likely be and started looking for me there. I crawled out from under the car I was hiding under and went into a bush. I hunkered down there until the men were scared away by the sirens."

"Did they say anything else?" the detective asked. "Can you give us anything that will help us find these guys?"

She hated the sound of impatience in his voice and wished she could tell him exactly who the men were, and why they'd been in her apartment. "They said they'd be back to get what they were looking for."

"There's no way in hell you're staying here tonight—or in the near future," Truck said firmly. "You can come and stay with me and Mary."

Macie was shaking her head before he'd finished his sentence. "I can't stay with you guys. You just got married!"

"Well, you're not staying here," Truck repeated. "Mace, they said they'd be back. It's not safe here."

She *knew* that. She was the one who'd had to jump out her window. She was the one who'd had to listen to the one guy talk about wanting to hurt her. She was the one who'd had to crawl around the parking lot to try to stay hidden.

For the first time in a long time, she was furious. At the situation, at Ford saying something she knew. But as soon as the feeling swept through her, she pushed it away. Anger was what had pushed her brother away all those years ago.

"She can stay with me," Colt said, successfully diverting Macie's attention.

"What?" she asked.

"That's a good idea," the detective said.

Macie looked from one man to the other, not sure what to say.

"Macie, look at me," Colt said quietly.

She turned to him.

"What do *you* want to do? What are you thinking?"

"I don't want to stay here," she blurted. "One of the guys was determined to get his hands on me, and not in a good way, if you know what I mean. But I don't want to stay with my brother because he and Mary just got back together again, and I don't want to mess that up. But I also don't want to make him mad by staying with *you*." Her voice dropped to barely a whisper. "The last time I got in a fight with him, I didn't see him again for almost twenty years."

And with that, Truck was at her side again. "Mace…what are you talking about?"

Macie bit her lip and couldn't look at him. She stared at his shoulder instead. "We fought before you left for the Army, and you were so mad at me you never came home. You didn't write or talk to me for years. I don't want to do anything to make you that mad at me ever again."

"Mercedes Laughlin," Truck said gently but sternly. "Look at me."

She didn't want to. She *really* didn't want to. She could already feel his condemnation. Her breaths sped up and she pinched her thigh again, trying to stave off another anxiety attack.

"Easy, Truck," Colt said.

"Macie," her brother said in a gentler tone, leaning closer but not touching her. "We fought the night before I left, but I was already over it by the next morning. Brothers and sisters fight. It happens. I was worried about you. You know I didn't like that guy you were seeing. But we were teenagers. And I wrote you. For *years*. But when I didn't hear anything back, I thought you were still mad at *me*."

Macie's head came up and she stared at her brother. "You did?"

"Yeah, Mace. I love you. I always have, and I always will. I even called. Several times. On Christmas. Your birthday. But Mom always told me you didn't want to talk to me," Truck said.

"I didn't know you called," she said in shock. "And I didn't get any letters."

Truck's face got hard then. "Damn our parents," he said under his breath.

"They said you never came home because of *me*. Because I was a terrible sister. Because of the—"

She caught herself and snapped her mouth shut at the last second.

"The what?" Truck asked.

Macie shook her head.

Truck sighed. "I was worried about you then, and I'm worried about you now. But I'm not mad at you. I just found you again; *nothing* is going to keep me from talking to you. From getting to know you better. I love you, sis."

"But you don't want me to stay with Colt. Why not?"

She watched as Ford took a deep breath. He looked over at Colt, then back to her. "You're my sister. No one is good enough for you. I don't like that I didn't know you guys had gotten…close, at my wedding."

Refusing to look at Colt, she somehow got up the nerve to ask, "Is he not a good person?"

She felt Colt squeeze her hand, but he didn't interrupt or otherwise put in his two cents.

"He's an amazing person," Truck said immediately. "I trust him with my life. I have no doubt that he'll take good care of you and make sure you're safe. But you're my *sister*. And I don't like the thought of you being with *any* man. I didn't like it when I was eighteen and you were dating that douchebag, and I don't like it now."

"I've dated," Macie told him. "In fact, I just broke up with a guy before your wedding."

"That's not the point—" Truck began.

"Actually," the detective interrupted. "I think that's a *great* point, and one I was going to get to. Who is he? What's his name? Could he have had anything to do with what happened tonight?"

Macie turned to look at the police officer. Amazingly, she'd forgotten he was sitting there listening. Her mind was still reeling with everything her brother had told her.

"Yeah, Mace. Who is he?" Truck asked, standing once more.

"We broke up a while ago." The last thing she wanted to do was talk about Teddy.

"What'd he do to you?" Truck growled.

Macie shook her head. She really *really* didn't want to discuss Teddy, especially not with Colt and her brother there. "Nothing."

"Hon," Colt said, "It's okay. We aren't going to judge you. We need to know if he had anything to do with this."

She looked down at her leg and almost laughed out loud. Not judge her? She felt as if every single person she met, every single day of her life, was judging her…and finding her wanting. Intellectually, she knew it was probably the anxiety messing with her head, but what if it wasn't? What if she really was an awful person?

She felt somewhat out of it after taking the Vistaril tablet, but not so out of it that she wanted to talk about what a colossal mistake she'd made in dating Teddy.

When no one said anything after a long pause, she sighed. They weren't going to give it up. It was better just to get it over with. "I met

Teddy online. He seemed nice. We started dating. He came over and watched movies with me a few times, but I never really felt comfortable with him. We went out for lunch one day, and I had an anxiety attack. He got embarrassed and left."

"He *left* you there? When you needed him? What an asshole," Colt said.

Macie looked up at him in surprise. His hand had tightened on hers and it was obvious that he was upset on her behalf.

"He came over later that night but I wouldn't let him in. I broke up with him. He was upset, but he left without protest. I haven't heard from him since."

"What was his last name?" the detective asked.

"Dorentes." Macie said.

"Theodore Dorentes?"

"Yeah."

The detective whistled long and low.

"What?" Truck asked. "Do you know him?"

"Yeah, you can say that," the detective said dryly. "Possession, possession with intent to distribute, assault, larceny, and disorderly conduct...to start with."

Macie sucked in a breath. "Seriously?"

"Seriously," the detective confirmed.

Macie turned to Colt. "I didn't know. I swear I didn't know." Then she turned to her brother. "I didn't!"

"Shhhh, we know you didn't," Colt soothed.

"Okay, so I think we know who ordered her house broken into," the detective said dryly. "The question is why. What was he looking for?"

All three men looked at Macie.

She gulped and shrugged. "He was only here a few times."

"He obviously stashed something somewhere," Truck said.

Macie felt her chest getting tight and her fingers began to tingle once more. She looked around and didn't see anything that looked out of place. "What? Where? I haven't seen anything."

"He probably hid it so you *wouldn't* find it. Thought he could get it next time he came over, but then you broke up with him," the detective mused.

"There are drugs in my apartment?" she practically screeched. So much for her anti-anxiety meds working.

"Why take so long to come back?" Truck asked.

The detective shrugged. "No clue. Maybe it wasn't important until now. It makes sense that he knew about her safe room. I'm assuming you told him about it?" he asked Macie.

"No! I hadn't been dating him that long," she said vehemently. "But..." Her voice trailed off.

"But what?" Colt asked.

Macie sighed. "One time when he was over I got up to get us something to drink and Teddy said that he needed to use the restroom. He was gone a really long time and I just figured he was having...you know...stomach issues. I didn't want to embarrass him so I didn't say anything about it."

"He was probably snooping around looking for somewhere to stash whatever he wanted to hide. I'm guessing he was under pressure from another dealer and was desperate," the detective said. "Then when Macie broke up with him he didn't have an opportunity to get back into her room to collect his stuff."

Macie shivered thinking about Teddy snooping around her place and finding her safe room. She wasn't sure she'd ever feel safe again.

"I think we're done here," Colt said. "Macie's about at the end of her rope. Truck, can you drive her car to Killeen? I can take her with me."

Truck eyed his commanding officer for a heartbeat, and Macie thought they might start arguing right there, but eventually he gave a quick nod.

"You have nothing to worry about," Colt told him. "Nothing is going to happen to your sister."

"It better not," Truck said under his breath. Then he kneeled next to Macie once more. He put his hand on her thigh, and the weight and heat of it felt good on her chilly skin. "Thank you for calling me tonight, Mace. I'm so glad you're all right."

"Thank you for coming," she said.

"Anytime you need me, I'm here," he responded. "And I know this will be impossible, but I'm asking anyway—forget *everything* our parents told you about me and about what happened back then. Not one fucking word was true. They are awful human beings, and I hate like hell that I didn't try harder to stay connected with you. My only excuse is that I was young and dumb and didn't want anything more to do with them. I'm ashamed that I thought for even one second that you might've had a good reason for not wanting to talk to me. I shouldn't have let my feelings about them interfere with my relationship with you. And for that, I'll forever be ashamed of myself."

Macie's eyes filled with tears. He was right, it was impossible to block out the years of hurtful words her parents had hurled at her. But she hated that he felt responsible for what happened.

"I should've come and seen you when you were injured." Her eyes went to the gnarly scar on her brother's face. "I didn't think you'd want to see me. But you should know I cut off all ties with Mom and Dad when they got home from visiting you. They said some truly horrible stuff, and even though it was one of the hardest things I'd ever done, I told them that they were dead to me. I haven't spoken to them since."

Truck's eyes closed for a second before he nodded. He stood and kissed the top of Macie's head. "I'll bring Mary over to see you tomorrow."

"I'm not sure—" Colt started, but Truck interrupted him.

"Tomorrow," he repeated firmly.

Macie looked from Colt to her brother, then back to Colt. He finally nodded.

"I'll call Ghost and have him pick me up at your house after I drop off Macie's car," Truck said, then he turned and headed for the front door of the apartment.

"After we check out this safe room of yours, my guys will be about done looking around," the detective said, standing as well. "I think it goes without saying that if you find anything that doesn't belong, don't touch it and *call* me."

Macie was nodding when Colt said, "We will. Thank you."

Colt looked down at her. "You ready to go pack? I want to look at those scrapes too. Get them cleaned up before we get out of here."

Macie swallowed hard and took a deep breath. Her head hurt and her fingers were still tingling, but the thought of going home with Colt comforted her. She stood up and swayed on her feet. She clutched the blanket around her shoulders when she'd sat down to talk to the detective and closed her eyes.

"Easy, Mace." Picking her up as if she weighed no more than a child, Colt headed for the hallway which led to her bedroom.

Instead of worrying about whether or not he would drop her or where she should put her hands, Macie lay her head on his shoulder and kept her eyes shut.

It had been a long time, maybe forever, since she'd felt as calm as she did right now. Some of it had to do with the meds she'd taken earlier, but most of it was Colt. There was something about him that made her feel more grounded.

Chapter Three

Colt did his best to control his anger. He was pissed way the hell off. When he got his hands on this Teddy person, he was going to wish that he'd simply walked away from Macie. Seeing her hunched over in the chair and worried that Truck was going to leave and not talk to her again made him want to punch something.

He didn't know her parents, but he hated them all the same.

He knew he had to get a handle on his emotions or he was going to worry Macie even more than she already was. He'd talked to his aunt about his cousin's anxiety issues. There was a lot he didn't understand, but he did know that this wasn't something Macie could control. She'd constantly worry about any and everything.

But he had no problem reassuring her when she needed it. Being anxious wasn't a deal breaker for him. From what little he knew about her, she was an amazing person. He'd looked at some of the websites she'd designed and was highly impressed. She was creative and generous, and he would do what he could to protect her from anything that might cause her distress in the future.

When he'd started thinking long term, Colt didn't know, but he also wasn't stressed out about it either. He'd connected with Macie when she'd been at his house after Truck and Mary's wedding. He'd thought he'd have time to feed her breakfast and get her number so they could continue to get to know each other. At some point, he was going to have to ask why she'd left the way she had…but right now wasn't the time.

He sat Macie gently on the counter in her bathroom. He leaned close and placed his hands on the cool tiles next to her hips and waited for her to open her eyes. It took several moments, but when she finally brought her beautiful brown eyes up to his, he wasn't prepared for the jolt of electricity he felt.

Bringing one hand to her cheek, he was encouraged when she tilted her head and rested it on his palm. "You okay?" he asked softly.

She nodded and said, "No."

He smiled at the contradiction. But he had a feeling she was being completely honest. "Where is your first-aid stuff?"

She lifted her head and gestured to a cabinet behind him.

Colt got to work getting the Band-Aids and hydrogen peroxide ready. When he turned around again, he had to take a deep breath. He'd purposely kept his mind off the fact that she was wearing only a tank top and a pair of short-shorts. But she'd dropped the blanket, and he couldn't stop his eyes from tracking from her feet up her long legs to her curvy thighs. Her belly wasn't flat, but she wasn't overweight either. And her tits were lush and full. Even as he stared at her, he saw her nipples tighten under the cotton.

He finally looked up and saw she was examining him just as openly. Waiting until her gaze had traveled the length of his body, he finally said, "Let's get you cleaned up so we can get out of here."

She blushed when she looked up at him, but nodded.

Turning his thoughts away from how sexy he found her—but loving that she seemed to be just as interested in checking him out as he was her—Colt concentrated on cleaning the scrapes on her body. He put the bottle down on the counter and picked up one of her hands. The palm was scraped and red, and he hated knowing it was because she'd leapt out her fucking window into a tree. He hated every single bruise and mark on her smooth skin. Throughout his ministrations, she didn't cry and didn't make a sound. He knew he had to be hurting her, but she was stoic and calm as he tended to her wounds.

When he was finally satisfied that he'd cleaned the worst of her scratches, he helped her stand and wrapped the blanket back around her shoulders. "You need help packing?"

She considered his offer for a second, then shook her head. "How long will I be staying with you?"

Forever was on the tip of his tongue, but he held back the word, knowing it would stress her out...and that it was crazy. "At least a couple days. We need to give the detective time to find Teddy and find out what this is all about. The police department will increase patrols of the area, but they can't be here every minute. Those assholes who were here tonight *will* probably come back, and I don't want you anywhere near here when they do."

"Okay," she said a bit hollowly.

Colt wasn't too concerned about her tone; he had a feeling the pill she'd taken earlier was finally kicking in. She walked to the doorway of the bathroom, then turned back.

"Um...while I'm changing and packing some clothes, will you do me a favor?"

"Anything," Colt said immediately.

That got a smile out of her. "What if I asked for something crazy?" she retorted, with a tilt of her head.

"I'd do what I could to do whatever you needed," Colt told her.

She shook her head and a small smile curved her lips. He loved that he could make her smile after everything she'd been through.

"What do you need, hon?"

"In my safe room is a box. Will you get it for me? I'd like to take it with me...if that's okay."

"Of course it is. Can I ask what's in it?" He was planning on checking out this safe room of hers anyway. He knew the cops had checked it for anything Teddy might've left, but he wanted to look at it himself as well.

"It's nothing expensive or illegal," she said. "It's just a shoebox of keepsakes. Stuff from when I was younger and from college and stuff." She shrugged. "It's not a big deal, but I'd rather it not get destroyed if those guys come back."

Colt was curious as to what keepsakes she had that meant so much to her, but he didn't want to push. "Anything else?"

"Can I bring my computer? And my work files? Oh, and there's a box of CDs and my headphones in the other room that I'd love to bring with me, if possible."

Colt smiled bigger now. "No problem. What else?" He actually hoped she'd continue to list her most prized possessions, because the more stuff she moved over to his house, the more comfortable she'd be there. And the more comfortable she was, the less she'd feel inclined to come back to *this* place. As far as he was concerned, she could move her entire fucking apartment. He had plenty of room for her things. For her.

"Um…" She looked into the bedroom then back at him. "I'm not sure."

Colt walked up to Macie and put his hands on her shoulders. "Whatever you want to take with you is fine with me. If there's not enough room in my Wrangler, we can come back tomorrow."

"Why are you being so nice to me?" Macie asked, her brows drawn down in confusion.

"Because I like you, Macie Laughlin. You didn't do anything for this to happen to you tonight. I want to make sure you're as comfortable as you can be in my house. I know it will be stressful for you, and I want to mitigate that as much as I can."

"Oh."

He could tell she was still unsure. So he added, "And because you're Truck's sister. And all the men under my command are like brothers to me."

She nodded, as if that response made more sense than him liking her.

"Go pack," he ordered gently, turning her around to face the bedroom. "I'll grab the box from your safe room, which I can't wait to see, by the way. Then I'll go and pack up your computer and CDs. You change, and call me when you're done. I'll come back and grab your suitcase so you don't further hurt those hands. Okay?"

"I can carry my suitcase," she protested.

"Hon, I said I've got it. There'll be plenty of times in the future when I'll let you carry your own shit, but tonight isn't one of them. Got it?"

She studied him, but eventually nodded. "Can I ask something else?"

"Of course."

"Why were you up and with my brother when I called? Did I interrupt something important?"

He had a feeling she'd been worrying about that. "My two teams of soldiers just got back from a mission tonight. We were debriefing."

Her eyes widened in horror. "I interrupted you working?"

Colt couldn't have stopped himself if someone had a gun to his head. He leaned down and covered her lips with his own in a brief caress. He rested his forehead on hers and linked his fingers together at the small of her back. He felt his heart jolt when her hands landed on his chest, but she didn't push him away.

"You didn't interrupt anything," he told her. "We were almost done. But even if we weren't, you're more important than work. I don't care what time it is or what you think I'm doing, if you need something, you call. Got it?"

She didn't answer for a long time, and Colt lifted his head to stare at her. "Got it?" he repeated.

"I can't promise. I mean, you know how I am. I'll worry that I'm interrupting you, or that you'll be annoyed, or that your *boss* will be annoyed. And that you'll think I'm being stupid or weak."

"Macie, I won't—"

She cut him off. "So I can't promise to *always* call, but if it's a true emergency, as it was tonight, I'll call."

Colt wanted to protest. But it was a big deal for her to tell him what she was feeling. What her anxiety made her feel. "Okay, hon. But would you mind if I called *you* when I needed something?"

"You want to call me?"

"Yeah, Mace. There might be times when I need help with something. But, like you, I don't want to interrupt you if you're working or doing something important."

"You can call me," she said softly. "I don't think anything I do is nearly as important as what you do."

"I'm sure the authors and other people you work for would disagree. I've seen some of the websites you designed. That couldn't have been easy, and I know that you also keep them updated as well. I *know* that can get crazy, considering how fast some authors write."

That earned him another small smile.

Forcing himself to step back, he gestured to the bedroom. "Do not carry that suitcase yourself. I'll be back here in a bit. Okay?"

"Okay. Colt?"

He smiled. "Yeah?"

"Thanks. I was really scared tonight."

"I'm glad I was there," Colt said simply, then forced himself to turn and leave her to change and pack. If he stood there any longer, there was no telling what would pop out of his mouth. He was a seasoned soldier. Had seen and done way more shit in his life than anyone should ever have to. He wasn't proud of some of his actions in the past, but he couldn't change what he'd done.

But it was the thought of arriving to find Macie dead that haunted him more than any of the carnage he'd lived through did.

He left her in her bathroom packing up her toiletries and made a quick stop to her closet to grab the shoebox she referenced. Her safe room was just what she said it was, a small quiet space with a sleeping bag rolled up at one end. He found the box she wanted and headed out to the living room.

As he began to gather up the CDs strewn around her laptop on her desk in the main part of the apartment, Colt's mind spun with plans. He wanted to make his house a safe place for Macie. Wanted her to feel relaxed and to do whatever it took to minimize her anxiety when she was there. The safer she felt, the more comfortable she would be. And the more comfortable she was, hopefully the more receptive she'd be to dating him on a long-term basis.

He didn't know what he'd done the night of Truck's wedding to make her back off, especially when things had seemed to go so well, but now that he had a second chance, he wasn't going to blow it.

Chapter Four

Macie nervously rubbed her hands on her jeans as she waited for Mary and the others to arrive. She hadn't seen her brother's wife since their wedding day, and while she liked the other woman, she had a tendency to be extremely blunt. In some ways it was refreshing. Macie never had to wonder what Mary was thinking. But on the other hand, she was terrified of doing something that would irritate her sister-in-law and make her not like her anymore.

Colt had put off the visit for almost a week, which Macie was super grateful for. She'd seen Truck several times; he'd come over to his commander's house to make sure she was doing all right. He'd also gone back over to her apartment to grab more clothes and other odds and ends for her.

She'd barely left Colt's house in a week, but she was more than all right with that. He went to work each morning, but came home for lunch to check on her, and was home by three-thirty every afternoon. He'd explained that since the men under his command had just gotten back from an intense two-week mission, and he'd been monitoring their movements almost twenty-four seven, he had some flexibility on when he had to be in the office.

She didn't like hearing about her brother's mission. Not that Colt actually told her much, but just knowing he'd been overseas doing something dangerous was more than enough for her to worry.

The view from the table she was using at Colt's house was just as nice as the one from her apartment. She sat at the table in his dining room, which overlooked a small park in the neighborhood. Macie had always wanted kids. Always. But before now, she'd stayed away from them because it was too painful. At the moment, however, she found herself staring at the children on the playground for hours. They looked so carefree. So happy. She couldn't remember a time in her life when she was truly that relaxed. Maybe before Ford had left for the Army.

Thinking about her brother leaving—and what had happened afterward—made her anxiety flare. She had no idea how he could still care about her after she'd not returned his letters. She didn't know he'd sent them, but still. It had already been a long time since she'd talked to her parents, but she made a mental vow to never see them again. She'd never forgive them. And not just because they'd purposely kept Ford out of her life.

The doorbell rang, and Macie jumped. Looking at the clock, she saw it was three. Forcing herself to her feet, she went to the front door. She looked through the peephole, saw that it was Mary and the others, and took a deep breath. Colt wasn't here—he said he'd be home as soon as he could—so it was just her. Macie's heart raced and she crossed her arms and pinched her biceps, trying to keep her anxiety under control. This was her sister-in-law. It was fine.

"Mace!" Mary said happily as soon as the door was open. "It's about time!"

Macie opened the door wider to let Mary and the others in. She recognized them, but Mary went ahead and introduced them anyway. "I'm sure you remember, but this is my best friend, Rayne. Behind her is Emily and her daughter, Annie, and Casey. The others wanted to come too, but they were busy. We'll have to plan another get-together with them soon."

Macie smiled at the other women and closed the door behind them once they'd all entered. She gestured to the living room and bit her lip as she followed. She hadn't made anything for them to eat. She probably should've. Especially for Annie. Children were always hungry, weren't they? She should've made cookies. That would've been easy.

And crap. Her stuff was strewn all over the dining room table. She was used to it just being her and Colt, and he'd told her to leave her computer set up at the table, and they'd been eating in the living room on the couch while they watched TV.

Macie was working her way to a full-blown anxiety attack when she felt a small hand slip into her own. Looking down, she saw Annie staring at her with a big smile. Her hair was messy around her head, but the little girl didn't seem to notice or care. She was wearing a pair of jeans that had dirt on the knees and a pink T-shirt with white sequins all over it. Squinting, Macie saw that it said "I like glitter."

Annie saw her looking at it and smiled. "Like my shirt?"

"It's cute," Macie told her.

Annie's nose wrinkled, and she said, "Look what it can do!" And with that, she ran her free hand down her chest and the sequins changed directions and colors. Now they were brown and said, "But dirt is cool too."

Macie smiled. "That's funny."

"I wish the dirt part was what showed all the time," Annie pouted.

"Annie, what did we talk about?" Emily reprimanded gently.

The little girl looked at her mom. "That I should just say thank you when people give me a compliment. But Macie is my friend, I can tell her secrets."

Macie glanced at Annie in surprise. "I've only met you once. At the wedding."

Annie looked at her with big blue eyes and said, "But you're Truck's sister. And he's my favorite uncle. And my brother is named after him. So that means you're my aunt. And thus, we're friends."

Macie's eyes teared up, and she had to look away from the little girl before she lost it completely. For the millionth time in her life, she regretted being so weak. For letting her parents coerce her into the worst decision of her life.

"Thus?" Mary questioned with a laugh.

"She's been reading a lot," Emily said. "It's her new favorite word."

"I'm glad we're friends," Macie told Annie.

"Me too," Annie answered happily.

It had been a long time since Macie felt accepted so readily and without strings. Annie was able to make her feel comfortable in a way she rarely felt around others...children included.

"Where's your brother?" she asked the little girl.

"Daddy and him are having a manly bonding moment and I wasn't invited," Annie pouted.

Macie looked at Emily.

The other woman laughed and explained, "I needed a break. Ethan doesn't sleep much. So Fletch took him to the office for the afternoon."

"I wanted to go to the office too," Annie said dejectedly. "I wanted some manly bonding time too." Then she perked up. "But I also wanted to come see you. So here I am!"

Macie squeezed Annie's hand. "I'm glad."

"I've never been in the commander's house," Casey mused.

"Me either," Rayne said. "And I've known him the longest."

"It's nice," Mary noted. "It feels comfortable."

"Why do you sound surprised?" Emily asked.

Mary shrugged. "I don't know. I mean, I guess because it's the commander. He's always seemed so stern. So cold."

"He's not cold," Macie said, surprised that anyone could think Colt was stern. "He's amazing. Patient and kind. He'd never hurt a fly." She regretted her words when three pairs of eyes stared at her in surprise. "What? He's *not* nice?" she asked quietly.

"Annie, do you want to go play?" Emily asked. "There's a playground right across the street."

"Yes!" the little girl shouted, then got serious. "But don't talk about anything important. I don't want to miss anything."

Macie forced a smile and squeezed Annie's hand once more. "We won't."

"Stay at the playground. I'll be watching from here. If you wander off, I'll take away your obstacle course privileges for a month," Emily warned.

Annie snapped to attention and dropped Macie's hand as she saluted her mom. "I won't, Mommy. Promise. Bye!" And with that, she ran to the front door and disappeared. They all watched as, seconds later, she ran onto the playground and immediately started playing with a group of boys.

"She is way too addicted to that obstacle course," Mary said wryly.

"I know, but it makes an affective punishment to take it away, so I'm not complaining," Emily said with a smile.

"Obstacle course?" Macie asked.

"The guys have a course they use at work for PT sometimes. Fletch took Annie there one day and that was that. She didn't want to do anything else. And she's good at it too. Fast."

Macie had met Fletch and the other men Ford worked with at the wedding. She loved how protective and loving they were with their wives. It was part of the reason she'd had such a major anxiety attack at the reception. She wanted the same. And knew she was too broken to ever have a man like that. A man who could put up with her insecurities and anxiety for the long haul.

"Let's sit," Rayne said, gesturing to the couches.

Macie knew she should be offering everyone something to drink, but she couldn't remember what was in Colt's fridge. What if she offered colas or juice and he didn't have any? Should she offer to see if he had any beer or wine? She was getting overwhelmed, so she kept quiet and followed the others to the living room to sit down.

No one said anything for a moment, and Macie's anxiety spiked. She should say something. Get the conversation rolling...but what should she say? She wasn't a part of these women's lives, even if Ford *was* her brother.

"What do you know about Colt?" Mary asked, as blunt as ever.

Macie blinked. "Um...he's my brother's commander. He's in charge of another group of soldiers too. He manages stuff from here while they go on missions." Said out loud, it sounded ridiculous.

But no one seemed to think her explanation was weird or stupid.

"Right," Mary said. "But do you know why he was chosen as their commander?"

Macie shook her head. "Because he was qualified?"

Mary chuckled. "You could say that. Look, we all like the commander. He's an amazing man, and he's kept our husbands safe more times than we can count. But...he's not exactly... What word did you use...kind?"

Macie stared at her sister-in-law. "Yes he is," she countered.

Mary shook her head. "I'm trying to look out for you. He's got a reputation for being one of the toughest officers on post. He doesn't like excuses, and doesn't like it when his soldiers are late and I heard that when he was at another post, he refused to let a soldier take leave when his baby was being born. I also heard that once he—"

"No," Macie said firmly.

"No, what?" Mary asked.

"I appreciate that you're trying to look out for me, but there's no need," Macie said, trying to sound firm. She knew Mary had a tendency to say whatever she was thinking, but she didn't want to hear gossip about Colt.

Mary's voice gentled. "I'm not trying to be a bitch, I swear. I just think you need to know so you don't have expectations that might never be met. The commander was a Delta Force soldier himself, Macie. He actually left the teams after an incident where one of his teammates was captured. I heard Truck talking about it on the phone one night with Blade. He said the commander went crazy. That he killed forty-two people that day."

"Have you ever been so worried about something you can't breathe?" Macie asked Mary out of the blue.

"What?"

"Have you stood in a room and known deep in your soul that *everyone* was talking about you behind your back?"

"No, but—"

"I know you've been through a lot, Mary. I *know*. There's a saying I try to live by: everyone you meet is fighting an invisible battle you know nothing about, so you should always be kind. I think you and I know more about that than anyone else in this room. If I told you that Truck was an asshole, would you believe me? Would that change how you feel about him?"

"You know it wouldn't," Mary said.

"Right. I can't pretend to know how Colt was feeling when he killed those people. I would imagine he was angry. And scared for his friend. And frustrated, and a hundred other emotions I can't name. How would you feel if *you* were that captured soldier? Wouldn't you want your fellow soldiers to do whatever it took to get to you? What if that was Rayne, and someone was holding her hostage? Wouldn't you kill forty-two people to get to her?

"The night of your wedding reception was a living hell for me. I was pretending to be happy, but I was miserable and freaked out that everyone was staring at me, wondering who I was and why I was there. Colt was the *only* one who noticed. He understood something was wrong and he got me out of there. Spent the entire night making sure I was okay. He didn't pressure me for sex. In fact, not once did I even worry that might be why he was helping me. He held me in his arms all night, making me feel safe, even as I struggled with my brain telling me things that I knew damn well weren't true, about everyone staring at me at your reception.

"I don't give a shit what Colt did in the past. Just as I don't care what *you* did. You aren't perfect either, and what you just told me was rude and bitchy, but I'm going to let it go because I want to be your friend, you're married to my brother and I truly believe you were trying to help me. I don't expect Colt to be some sort of paragon. The bottom line is that he's kind to *me*—and that's what I care about. He's also truly concerned about the men under his command, including my brother, your husband. And when I called last week, freaked out and scared because men broke into my apartment, Colt was the one who got me through that situation. He kept me calm so the men didn't find me. I know *exactly* who Colt Robinson is. I think it's *you* who doesn't."

The silence in the room after her outburst was oppressive, but Macie refused to look away from Mary. It took everything she had to do it, but she held eye contact with her.

"I'm sorry," Mary said quietly. "God, you're right. I was out way of line. But in my defense, I was doing it because I care about you. Because I like you. I'm trying to stop saying whatever I'm thinking, but I'm obviously failing. Forgive me?"

"Of course I do," Macie told her. The last thing she wanted was to fight with her sister-in-law.

"I'm sorry you were uncomfortable at the reception," Casey said. "Was it something someone said?"

Macie took a deep breath. She could either confess about her condition or make up something to blow off the other woman's concern. But she wanted friends. Wanted to be able to open up to them when something good *or* bad happened in her life. If she lied now, it would be almost impossible to explain later.

Making a split-second decision, she said, "I have chronic anxiety. I take meds for it, but sometimes they don't always help." She kept the explanation simple, and held her breath to see how they'd react.

"That sucks," Casey said.

"Wow, I can't imagine how hard that would be," Rayne commented.

But it was Mary who blew her mind. She got up out of the chair she'd been sitting in and came over to Macie. She knelt in front of her and put a hand on her knee. "I'm sorry," Mary said. "I should know better than anyone not to assume things about people. And for the record, you seem as if you always have everything under perfect control.

Yeah, you were nervous that day you came to the bank, but I figured it was because you hadn't met me before."

"I went home after that meeting, took a pill I only use in extreme situations, and slept for twelve hours," Macie admitted.

"For what it's worth, I admire you," Mary said. "You've been through hell and you haven't let it beat you. You're tough as nails."

Macie gaped at her. She knew what Mary had been through. Not only her childhood, but with the breast cancer she'd fought...twice. There was no way she thought *Macie* was tough. Most days, she felt like a wreck.

"But I can see it now. You're perfect for the commander."

All sorts of things raced through Macie's head at that comment. That she was perfect for him because she needed taking care of. That she was too weak to get by without a man at her side. But then Mary continued.

"Because your heart is so big, you see the good in anyone. And you worry about things because you care. Too much. I think the commander needs that. He needs someone to care about him the way he cares about all the soldiers under his command."

Macie blinked. Mary was exactly right when it came to Colt. He worked hard. Worried about the soldiers under his command...and their families.

She thought about the last week, how happy he'd been when she'd made dinner for them. When she'd done laundry. When she'd changed the sheets on the bed they'd been sleeping on all week. She'd thought he was being grateful because he was trying to make her feel better about living there temporarily, but she realized now that he'd probably always had to do those things himself.

"Shit," Casey said, wiping tears from under her eyes. "You guys are making me cry. Bitches."

Mary smiled at Macie, then turned to Casey. "That's us. The bitch squad."

Macie couldn't believe she thought someone calling her a bitch was funny. In the past, the insinuation could send her to bed for a few days. But it felt like a compliment to be compared to Mary, who never took shit from anyone. Macie liked her. Ford had talked to her a lot about Mary's background, and had warned her not to take what she said personally. He'd told her that his wife was brash, but it was only to guard herself from being hurt. It made sense then, and it made even more sense now.

She wasn't mad at Mary for saying what she had about Colt. The other woman had been trying to look out for Macie. But the thing was that she didn't give a shit what Colt had done in the past. She didn't know the details of what had happened, but she trusted Colt. Knew he wouldn't hurt anyone if the situation didn't call for it. And curiously enough, what Mary said made Macie feel even safer with Colt. He'd make sure her ex didn't get anywhere near her. Of that she had no doubt.

"Have they found the men who broke into your house, or your ex?" Rayne asked, as if she could read Macie's mind.

"Not yet. Truck went to my apartment the day before yesterday and realized that someone had been in there. They didn't trash the place, but they'd definitely been looking for whatever it was that Teddy had left. The cops didn't find anything in my safe room where Teddy told the guys whatever it was would be," Macie told them, already feeling more comfortable with these women than she had with anyone in a very long time.

"Holy crap!" Mary exclaimed.

"Drugs?" Casey asked.

"That's just it. I don't know. The cops brought a drug-sniffing dog to my place and he didn't find anything. He alerted to a few different places, but the handler thinks it was because Teddy had been there and probably had drugs with him when he was." Macie hated that he'd been in her place and might have had drugs on him, but she was trying to move past that. Colt had been a big help in that arena, reminding her that *she* wasn't the one doing drugs, and that she didn't know what Teddy had been doing.

"Do you need us to go to your apartment and clean up, or get you anything?" Emily asked.

Macie stared at her incredulously.

"What?" Emily asked when Macie didn't answer her question. "Should I not have asked? Does it make you anxious when people are in your space?"

Macie shook her head. "No. I mean, yes, but that's not...you don't know me," she blurted, stumbling over her words.

Emily smiled. "I know you're very important to the commander. I know that he requested our men ask us to come over today because he was worried you were here most days by yourself. I know he told Fletch that he would be off this weekend because he was going to spend it with you. I might not know you that well yet, but I want to. Besides, going to Lampasas will get me out of the house and some peace and quiet for a while. I love my kids, but they exhaust me."

"I'm happy to help too," Casey added.

"Me too," Mary said with a grin.

"I…thank you," Macie said. "But I don't need anything. Truck got me some stuff the other day, and Colt went over there the other night. He said he wanted to make sure my fridge was cleaned out, but I think he was hoping to find one of the men who broke into my apartment lurking around."

"That sounds like something one of our men would do," Casey said with a smile.

Just then, Annie came back into the house. She was out of breath and talking a mile a minute. "Mommy! I made a new friend. Her name is Sam. That's short for Samantha. I taught her how to play soldier and I really like her!"

Emily smiled at her daughter and gave the other women a look as if to say "See? Exhausting."

"That's great, baby. Now, go wash your hands before you get dirt all over the commander's house. I saw a bathroom next to the kitchen."

Without a word, Annie spun and headed for the washroom to clean up.

The rest of the afternoon passed relatively smoothly. Macie was surprised at how comfortable she felt with the three women, but it definitely helped to have Annie there. Her presence kept anyone from bringing up anything that might be upsetting to the little girl. They laughed, gossiped, and talked about what it was like to be an Army wife.

Before she knew it, it was quarter to four and the front door was opening and Colt was home.

Macie looked up and smiled at him. He saw her and came straight to her side. He leaned down and kissed her on the cheek and straightened. "Hey."

"Hey," she replied.

"You look like you're having a good time," he observed.

Macie nodded.

"It doesn't smell like you've started anything for dinner?" He raised a brow, making the statement a question.

Macie frowned. "No, I hadn't thought about it yet. It'll be easy enough to make something though. Grilled chicken? Hamburgers?"

He smiled and ran a hand over her hair. "I have a craving for Chinese. I can go and pick it up. I just didn't want to bring anything home if you'd put in the effort to make us something already."

"Chinese sounds great."

Colt smiled at her. "Perfect. You stay and chat. I have some things I need to finish in my office upstairs. I'll come back in a bit and you can tell me what you want. Okay?"

"Okay."

And it wasn't until then that he turned and nodded at the other women. "Good to see you," he said politely.

Mary was staring at Colt as if she'd never seen him before. Casey and Emily smiled at him and returned his greeting.

"Hi," Annie said boisterously.

"Hey, Annie. How are you? Have you been practicing the obstacle course for the upcoming kids' contest?"

"Yes!" she shouted, and nodded her head so hard, Macie thought it would come right off her shoulders. "I can't wait! I took five seconds off my time the last time I did it."

Colt wandered over and put his hand on her shoulder. "I have no doubt you're going to win that trophy," he said seriously. "I think you can absolutely do whatever you want to."

"I want to be a doctor," she said. "And help soldiers when they get hurt on missions so they can come home to their families."

Macie blinked in surprise. Most eight-year-olds she'd come across still wanted to be ballerinas or actresses. Annie's goal was much more specific...and lofty.

"Anyone who's in your unit will be very lucky," Colt said solemnly. Then he turned, smiled at the others, winked at Macie, and headed upstairs to his office.

"Holy crap," Casey whispered.

"I take everything back that I said," Mary mused with a shake of her head.

"He only had eyes for you," Emily told Macie with a smile. "We might not've existed for all the attention he paid to us."

"He wasn't trying to be rude," Macie defended Colt. "He just wanted to make sure I was okay. I was nervous about today, and he knew it."

Mary shook her head. "He looks at you like Truck looks at me. Like Beatle looks at Casey and Fletch looks at Emily."

Macie wanted to protest. Wanted to deny Mary's words, but she couldn't. She'd seen the way her brother looked at Mary. She'd been at the wedding and seen how *all* the men on Colt's team treated their women. It was true. She'd gotten used to being the center of Colt's attention, and she'd convinced herself he was simply being polite. But deep down, she knew better. They had a connection. A deep one.

She didn't respond, just simply smiled.

"How does Daddy look at you, Mommy?" Annie asked with a confused tilt of her head.

Emily tousled her daughter's hair. "Like I'm his wife, of course."

Annie frowned. "I don't get it."

"You will, baby. When you're older."

Annie rolled her eyes. "You always say that."

"That's because it's true."

"Uh oh, Mommy! Look! It's Ethan time!" Annie said and pointed at Emily's shirt.

There were two wet patches on the front of it.

"Oh crap. You're right," Emily said, then looked up at the group in embarrassment. "He usually eats around this time and even though I pumped"—she gestured at herself—"my body is on the same schedule he is."

The others all laughed, but Macie could only look at Emily in horror. Not because she'd leaked through her shirt, but because if that was her, she would be embarrassed beyond belief. She wouldn't ever be able to face the other women again. She couldn't understand how Emily wasn't completely mortified.

"I should probably get going too," Casey said. "I've got papers to grade for tomorrow."

"And I just want to see my husband," Mary said with a smirk.

Macie walked the women to the door and said goodbye to Casey and Mary. Annie ran ahead to the car so she could start it, apparently one of her favorite things to do.

It was just her and Emily standing in the doorway, and Macie struggled to find something to say and not stare at the wet splotches on her shirt.

"I'm sorry if I embarrassed you," Emily said softly.

At that, Macie's eyes whipped up to hers. "What?"

"I can tell you're uncomfortable. And I'm sorry."

"I just…if that had happened to me, I would die of mortification. Then I'd have to take one of my strong pills and hole up in a dark room with my headphones on for the rest of the night."

Emily chuckled. "Having kids does wonders for my tolerance for embarrassment. Annie has a habit of saying the absolute worst thing at exactly the worst times. And Ethan is always hungry. If I don't feed him on schedule, he screams bloody murder. I've learned it's easier to just find a corner and feed him rather than try to calm him down. And let me tell you, people are *not* that comfortable with breast-feeding in public. And it's not like I just whip out my boob or anything." Emily shook her head. "Annie was so much easier than Ethan for some reason. Anyway, I just wanted to make sure you were okay."

"I'm okay, thank you," Macie told her. And surprisingly, she was. The fact that Emily wasn't upset over what happened with her body went a long way toward soothing Macie's own apprehension about it. It was a natural thing. It happened. "Thank you for coming over today. I had a good time."

"You sound surprised," Emily observed.

Macie shrugged. "I've had a hard time making friends."

"I don't know why. You're funny. You're kind. And you aren't afraid to stick up for your man…which in our circle goes a really long way."

Annie chose that moment to honk the horn a few times.

Emily laughed. "That's my cue. Thanks for having us." Then she leaned over and gave Macie a quick hug, careful not to crush their chests together. "We need to do it again soon. I'll be in touch. Bye!"

Macie didn't have a chance to get a word in before Emily was halfway down the sidewalk and yelling at Annie to hush and to get in the backseat.

Two words stuck out from everything Emily had said. "Your man."

Macie wanted to admit that Colt wasn't her man. That she was only staying with him until he thought it was safe for her to go back to her apartment in Lampasas. That he was simply looking after one of his soldiers' sisters.

She was afraid to think anything else. Especially since she'd left her number for him after the wedding and he hadn't bothered to call.

She waved at Annie as Emily pulled away and went back into the house and shut the door behind her, making sure to lock it. She turned to go back into the other room and screeched in surprise when she almost ran into Colt.

"Everything good?" he asked.

Macie nodded.

"No, Macie," he said as he put a hand on the side of her neck and leaned in. "Are you good?"

She couldn't help the small smile that broke out. "I'm good," she told him. "Really. I liked them. Annie is hysterical, and I loved getting to know Emily and Casey more."

"And Mary? Did she behave?"

Macie must've hesitated a moment too long, because Colt sighed and pulled back. He reached for her hand and pulled her into the living room. He sat on the couch and tugged Macie down onto his lap. He put his arms around her waist and held her firmly.

Macie stared at him in shock. They'd slept curled up next to each other every night, and Colt never hesitated to touch her, to caress her cheek or run a hand over her hair. But he'd never simply hauled her around before—at least, not since the night of the break-in—and she hadn't sat on anyone's lap since she was five years old.

Not sure where to put her hands, she rested them in her lap awkwardly.

"What'd she say?" Colt asked.

"Nothing."

"Mace," he said more gently. "I can tell she said something. I mean, it's Mary, she can't help herself, it's part of her charm." He smiled. "Now tell me, so I can reassure you about whatever it was, and then I'll go get us some dinner. I'm hungry."

It was the last bit that made Macie change her mind about telling him. She had a feeling he would sit there all night if she didn't spill. He was that stubborn. But his stubbornness was one of the many reasons she was crazy about him.

Pushing those feelings to the back of her mind, refusing to think about them right now, she said, "I'm sure she was exaggerating, or that she simply doesn't know the truth."

"About what?"

Taking a deep breath, Macie said, "She was just trying to make sure I knew what this was. What was happening here. And she told me about you killing a bunch of people when your friend was captured."

She felt Colt's thigh muscles tense under her butt, and it seemed as if the air in the room thickened with emotion.

Oh shit. Why had she told him? She should've made something up. She was such an idiot! Now he was going to tell her she couldn't stay at his house anymore, that he couldn't help her. She should've kept her big mouth shut!

Chapter Five

Colt felt Macie begin to tremble in his lap and did his best to relax his own muscles. But it was too late. He could tell by the way she'd hunched in on herself and the way she wouldn't meet his eyes.

He hated doing anything to make her anxiety flare, so he quickly tried to fix it. Her words had surprised him and brought back the memories of that awful day, the day that had changed his life forever.

Tightening his arms around her so she couldn't flee, he began speaking.

"I'm forty-three years old. I've been in the military almost my entire adult life. I have no idea what I'll do when they finally force me to retire. I've never been married. Don't have any children. I've made my share of mistakes in my life, and I won't lie to you, Macie. I've killed people. Lots of them. But if I had to do it again, I would. Every time."

He paused and took a deep breath. He wasn't sure he could relive what had happened at the end of his Delta Force career.

Then he felt Macie relax slightly against him. She put her head on his shoulder and tentatively put her arms around his neck. That was all it took to give him the courage to open up to her. She wasn't rejecting him. She knew the basics, and still she put her arms around him.

"My team was sent into a hostile town to meet with who we thought were loyal supporters. Our intel said they wanted to assist us in taking down the Taliban that had a toehold in that region. Honestly, we were losing the fight there and needed all the help we could get. The bigwigs thought it would be a good idea to use local strength to fight. So we went in. We were cautious and uneasy, but we were given a direct order, so in we went. I was in charge of my team, and so I was in the lead when an RPG—rocket-propelled grenade—came out of nowhere and decimated the building behind where we were standing. It collapsed right on top of us."

Macie inhaled harshly, but didn't speak. Colt could feel her fingers at the nape of his neck, caressing the short hairs there. He closed his eyes and took a minute to appreciate the feel of her body on his. How good her fingers felt.

"I woke up some time later. I'm not sure how much time had passed. I was completely buried under the stones and concrete of the building, but somehow hadn't been crushed because of the way the walls fell. I don't know if you remember after 9/11 that some people were found alive in one of the stairwells of the collapsed buildings?"

Macie nodded, so Colt continued.

"Yeah, well, that happened to me too. I was relatively unhurt, just sore, confused, and had a raging headache. I pushed the rubble off myself and crawled out. It was almost dark but I could still see all around me. Two of my teammates were lying dead, their heads crushed under rocks from the building. Another had been dragged out of the debris and stripped. Bud was naked, and he had bullet holes throughout his body and a huge puddle of blood around him. Back home, he had two kids and another on the way. I turned my head to puke, and met the eyes of another teammate, Randy. He was alive. Lying in the debris of the building, but his legs and pelvis were crushed and he was pinned under a huge block of concrete.

"I went to his side, and he told me what had happened to our last teammate I hadn't found yet. Randy had witnessed what had happened to everyone, but couldn't do a damn thing to help. He knew he was dying. Could feel it. He said that Sergeant Griswald had fought off the insurgents at first, trying to keep them at bay. He'd used all his bullets and was trying to reload when they overwhelmed him. Bud had shot at them from where he was also trapped under the rubble, but they dragged him out and beat the hell out of him. When he was almost unconscious, they stripped him and began shooting...just for fun.

Randy said it seemed like the entire town was there, watching, laughing, participating. Women, kids, men, old and young alike. When Bud was dead, they turned back to Gris. He'd been detained by five insurgents."

Colt huffed out a breath. "Took *five* of those fuckers to contain him. He was strong as an ox, and I can imagine that he was pissed way the hell off. Anyway, they tied a piece of rope around his neck and dragged him away. Randy said Gris had managed to get his hands under the rope, so he wasn't strangled as they dragged him in the dirt, but he didn't know where they'd taken Gris or what had happened to him.

"The last words Randy said to me were to tell his wife that he loved her, and that he was proud as hell to be hers. He died in the middle of that fucking miserable town and there was nothing I could do about it. No amount of first aid would put his legs back together or stop the bleeding. Looking around at the four dead men surrounding me, something snapped. I was *so* enraged that these men—my friends...husbands and fathers, brothers and sons—were dead.

"By now it was fully dark, and I searched through the rubble and found what weapons I could and went on the hunt for Gris. We'd all been trained how to withstand torture, and I hoped like hell the assholes hadn't just killed him outright as they had Bud.

"Every single person I came into contact with on my hunt for Gris, I killed. Some with my bare hands, so I didn't draw attention to myself. I didn't give them a chance to identify themselves, either. Randy said the entire town had participated in the death of my teammates—and they'd laughed while doing it. I showed no mercy for any of them.

"By the time I found Gris, I almost didn't recognize him. They'd stripped him naked like they had Bud, and had tied him to a stake on the back side of the town. He was barely conscious, but I could tell even from my hiding spot that he was still fighting to live. I'd collected various firearms from the people I'd killed on my way through the town and had quite the arsenal set up...including an RPG.

"I didn't hesitate. I aimed that thing at a group standing near Gris and fired. It was stupid. I could've killed Gris."

"But you didn't," Macie said with complete certainty.

Colt jolted under her. He'd been so lost in the memories in his head that he'd forgotten where he was. Forgotten that Macie was even there.

"To confirm what you heard, hon...yeah, I killed a lot of people. Old women, teenagers, adults. I don't regret it, and I'd do it again if I was in the same situation."

"What about Gris?" she asked softly.

"What about him?"

"Did he live?"

"Yeah, he lived. When the air cleared and after I picked off the remaining insurgents who hadn't fled after I'd fired the RPG, I got Gris off that fucking stake and got us the hell out of there."

"You have to be proud of that," she said.

"I might've gotten Gris home, but I left Randy, Bud, and the others there. The one rule we take very seriously is that we never leave anyone behind."

Macie sat up on his lap and turned toward him. She took his face in her hands and looked into his eyes. "You couldn't get Gris and yourself to safety and take their bodies too. They'd have understood, Colt. And I have a feeling, if they were anything like you or my brother, they'd kick your ass for even *thinking* about coming back for their bodies after you'd rescued Gris."

She was right. Randy had been very vocal when it came to safety. About not taking stupid risks. And Bud was completely laid-back. He got his nickname because in boot camp, the drill sergeant accused him of being high because he wasn't fazed by anything. Bud would simply shrug and say that Colt had done what he'd had to do to get Gris home.

Even though he knew she was right, it didn't ease the feelings of guilt he still carried.

"I understand feeling guilty about something," Macie said after she'd put her head back on his shoulder.

Colt immediately snapped out of his own head and focused on the woman in his lap. She was no longer loose in his arms. He could feel her muscles tighten even as she began speaking.

"There are so many things I feel guilty about in my life. I've made so many mistakes it's not even funny. Starting with arguing with my brother before he left."

"You guys were kids. You can't blame yourself for that," Colt said. He moved a hand to rub the small of her back and the other rested on her thigh and kneaded her flesh there lightly.

"I guess I don't blame myself, but I wish I'd listened to him."

Colt stilled.

"The boy I was dating was bad news. Ford knew it, but I thought the guy loved me. I guess I latched on to him as a replacement for the affection I knew I'd lose when Ford left. But he wasn't a good guy. He convinced me that he loved me, and we'd be together forever. I was so young…I thought we were going to get married. I let him convince me to sleep with him. And I…I got pregnant when I was fifteen."

Colt forced himself to breathe, but didn't interrupt.

"I wanted that baby so much," Macie said softly. "We began fighting more and I suspected he was seeing other girls behind my back, but I wanted to make things work so bad. I told him about the baby, and of course he broke up with me. Said he wasn't ready to be a father. Just up and left. I was heartbroken, but determined to raise my baby on my own."

She stopped speaking, and Colt gave her several minutes to continue, but when she didn't, he brought his hand to the back of her neck and massaged her. "What happened?" He was pretty sure she didn't have a child hidden somewhere. He did the math in his head and figured that her child would be somewhere around eighteen.

"My parents made me have an abortion."

Her words were flat, and all the more heartbreaking because of the lack of emotion in them.

"I'm so sorry, hon."

She curled farther into him, bringing her knees up. Colt tightened his embrace, trying to cocoon her with support.

"They said I'd make a horrible mother. Convinced me I had no way of supporting myself, never mind a baby. Said they wouldn't babysit and I'd have to drop out of school. They told me I was a slut and it was no wonder my brother left and hadn't spoken to me since. They said I had no common sense and my baby would probably be deformed or handicapped."

"Assholes!" The word burst from Colt before he could stop it. "Macie, how old you are has nothing to do with whether or not your baby will be born healthy. And I can guarantee that Truck didn't leave because of you."

"I know that…*now*. But I didn't then. I let them convince me it was for the best. They drove me to the clinic and refused to come back to see the doctor with me. When she was aborted…it hurt, Colt. Not physically, the doctor numbed me for that part of the procedure, but it felt as if a part of me was being torn away. The doctor said I was imagining it, that the fetus was small enough that I couldn't feel anything, but it was as if we were spiritually connected. I knew the second she died."

"She?" Colt asked, tears forming in his eyes as he imagined the mental anguish she'd gone through as a vulnerable teenager.

"Yeah. A daughter. She'd be eighteen. Graduating from high school and getting ready for college. I often wonder what kind of person she'd be today. Would she be a pain in the ass and sneaking out every night? Or would she be into math and science? Maybe she'd be an athlete or a singer. I feel guilty for giving in to my parents so easily. I should've stood up to them. Maybe today my daughter would be alive and getting ready to change the world."

"Listen to me," Colt said, turning her chin so she had to face him. "You have nothing to feel guilty about. *Nothing.* Your parents are the ones who should feel guilty. They treated you and Truck like shit for years. The fact that they did what they could to make you feel as if his leaving was your fault was already enough for me to hate them. But the fact that they made you abort your baby when you didn't want to is unforgivable.

"If I've learned anything over the years, it's that we can't go back. We can't change the past. We can only go forward. It sucks, and it's not fair, but it is what it is. You have your brother back now. You have me. You never have to speak to your sperm donors again. You have a whole group of men and women who are more than happy to be your friends.

"I won't say that I'll never look back at what happened to my friends and wish things could be different, but I'm doing my best to move on. To be the kind of man they'd want at their backs. To be the kind of commander who would never send his men into battle without knowing all the facts. Your brother and his team, and the other team I command, will never have to worry about whether they have all the facts before putting their lives on the line. I will *not* deploy them if I'm not sure I know everything there is to know about what I'm sending them into. Randy and Bud didn't die in vain. They live on in your brother, and in every single Delta Force team member I'm responsible for."

"What happened to Gris?" Macie asked.

Colt smiled for the first time in what seemed like hours. "He was medically retired. Lives in this tiny town called Stehekin in Washington state. The only way you can get there is by a four-hour ferry boat ride up

Lake Chelan. They don't have any big-box stores, there are only about a hundred year-round residents, and it's buried under snow seven months of the year."

"Sounds like heaven," Macie said with a smile.

"I've been there several times. And it is," Colt agreed. "He and his wife have three kids. His oldest son is named Colt."

Her smile grew even bigger. "I'd love to meet him sometime."

"Done. I'll gladly take you up to Stehekin. In the summer though. I don't like all that snow."

She giggled, and Colt could only stare at her. *He'd* done that. She'd just finished talking about her baby being killed and he'd made her giggle.

Colt had never been a believer in fate. There was no way Randy, Bud, and the others were meant to die how they did. No way that Gris was fated to be tortured like he was.

But sitting on his couch, with Macie relaxed and warm in his arms, he had to reconsider.

He'd done some shitty things in his life. He definitely didn't deserve someone like Macie. And yet, here she was. There were so many decisions the two of them had made over the years, and even one might have meant they never would've crossed paths. But they had.

Colt rearranged them on the couch so his back was against the arm and she was half-sitting, half-lying between his legs, and clicked on the television. They'd disclosed some pretty heavy things to each other today. It was time to rest and simply enjoy being with each other.

He felt Macie relax farther into him and eventually fall asleep. He nuzzled her hair and inhaled its floral scent. He vowed three things, right then and there.

One, if her parents ever tried to contact her, he'd make sure they understood that they were dead to her, and if they ever spoke to her again, they'd regret it. Second, he would not let her ex-boyfriend and his thugs lay one hand on her. She'd been through too much.

And three, he loved her and would do whatever it took to make her happy for the rest of her life. She was meant to be his. She hadn't blinked at his recounting of the way he'd slaughtered so many people to save one man. Hadn't been horrified, hadn't come up with excuses for his behavior.

"Love you, Mace," he said in a barely audible whisper.

"Mmmm," she murmured, and tightened her hold on his arm that was around her chest.

Colt smiled, and finally felt the guilt lift that he'd carried around with him for so long. Raising his eyes to the ceiling, he mouthed, *Thanks, guys.*

Chapter Six

Macie looked up from her computer in surprise when she heard the garage door open. Glancing at her watch, she saw it was only two in the afternoon. She wasn't expecting Colt home for another hour and a half or so. She wasn't panicked though, because it wasn't as if the thugs who'd broken into her apartment would open the garage door if they'd tracked her to Colt's house.

Thankful for the break—she'd been rebuilding an author's website after her old one had been infected with malware, and her eyes felt like they were crossed—Macie saved her work on the computer and stood to greet Colt. It was Friday afternoon, and she was looking forward to him being home for two full days. She felt grounded when he was there. As if he had some sort of magical force field around him that prevented her anxiety from flaring up.

She heard the door to the garage shut and then he was there.

"Hi."

"Hey, hon. How's your day been?"

"Good. Yours? You're home early."

"I am. I thought we could go on a trip this weekend, if you wanted to."

Macie froze. A trip? Together? Would they stay in the same hotel room?

It was a stupid thought. They'd been sleeping in Colt's bed together since she'd moved in. It wasn't sexual, and as the days passed, she got more and more unsatisfied with the status quo. She had no idea how to let Colt know she was ready for more. Didn't want to do anything that might change the comfortable relationship they had. And if she initiated sex, and he didn't want it, she'd be embarrassed and have to move back to her apartment.

As if he could sense her inner turmoil, Colt strode toward her. Macie loved seeing him in his uniform. He looked confident and strong, things that were the complete opposite of how she felt most of the time.

"If you'd rather, we can stay here like we did last weekend," he reassured her as he tucked a piece of hair behind her ear gently. "I just thought you could use a change of pace. You've been cooped up in my house almost since you moved in."

"I like your house," she blurted.

"I know you do, hon. And I like you *in* my house, but I'd like to take us both away for a weekend. The detective in Lampasas hasn't found Teddy yet, though after your place was broken into again, they've really stepped up their searches. I reserved a room at the Four Seasons in Austin. I requested a view of Lady Bird Lake and the Congress Avenue Bridge so we could watch the bats leave at dusk to go feed."

Macie had heard of the famous bats of Austin. It was said that over a million bats lived under the bridge and came out every night at dusk to feed. She'd wanted to go see the phenomenon, but hadn't ever made the time.

Colt went on. "They have an aquarium in Austin that we could do, or we could take a tour of the downtown area. Sixth Street is always an option too. They have a huge multi-block party every weekend, complete with live bands, but I wasn't sure that would be your thing. The stores down there are pretty eclectic, and we could wander around during the day if you wanted. The bottom line is that I just want to spend time with you, Macie. One on one. Continue to get to know you. Have some fun."

Macie took a deep breath and nodded. "I'd like that."

"But?" Colt asked.

Macie smiled a little and shook her head. "How can you read me so well?"

"Because I pay attention. What part of my plans do you not like? Nothing is set in stone. We can change things up however you want."

"There's a store called Uncommon Objects in Austin. One of the authors I work for told me about it. It's an antique store, but it's apparently so much more than that. They have all sorts of stuff, but what I'd really like to get my hands on are the antique photos. Real photos of real people. Memories that are lost to those who experienced them, but I can only imagine the stories that will run through my head when I see them."

Colt was smiling at her and had a look in his eyes that she couldn't interpret. "Of course we can go there."

"And there's a restaurant called Bacon that I want to go to. I saw a rerun of an episode of *Food Paradise* on the Travel Channel that featured it. They make all different kinds of flavored bacon. I think it would be fun to visit."

The indulgent look hadn't left Colt's face. "I've been there. And you're right, the food is amazing. But hon, I have bad news."

"What?" Macie asked.

"They closed."

"Seriously?"

"Yeah. A couple years ago. I guess the street it was on frequently flooded, and they got tired of it. They were supposed to open in a new location, but I haven't heard if they've done that or not."

"Well, darn," Macie said.

"I'll make you bacon if you want it, Mace," Colt told her.

"It won't be the same," she said with a pout.

Colt chuckled. "True. We'll see if we can find another place that sells kick-ass bacon while we're there. How's that? The city's well known for their eclectic, independently run restaurants."

"Okay."

"So you'll go with me?"

Macie looked up at Colt and said seriously, "I think I'd go anywhere with you."

"We won't have time to get there to see the bats tonight, and I figure we'll both be tired by the time we arrive. So I thought we could just order room service."

"Sounds perfect. Colt?"

"Yeah, Mace?"

"I appreciate everything you've done for me. I mean, I know I'm Ford's sister and he's one of the soldiers under your command, but I appreciate it all the same."

He looked confused then. "Macie, you know I'm not he ing you just because you're Truck's sister, right?"

Macie heard the incredulity in his voice, and began to get n rvous in a way she hadn't felt around him since she'd moved in. " /ell, no, because that would be crazy. I mean, you can't move *everyone* siblings into your house if they need help. But I get that you were t ere with Ford when I called him that night. And when I refused to s y at his place with him and Mary, you were put in a weird spot. All I'm saying is that I'm thankful."

She couldn't interpret the look on his face now, and hat was beginning to freak Macie out. She'd obviously said the wro g thing, *again*, but didn't know how to fix it. So she tried to fill the wkward silence.

"I mean, it's not like we aren't friends, because I think we re. I like you, and I think you like *me*. But when you didn't call after my rother's wedding, I kinda figured out where we stood with each other and I'm okay with that."

"When I didn't call?" Colt asked, breaking his weird silenc . "Mace, I didn't have your number. I could've asked Truck, but I didn know if that's what *you* wanted. I also didn't want you to feel weird ab ut what happened that night…but I sure didn't. I loved talking to you Getting to know you. But I wasn't going to force you to go out with e if you didn't want to."

"I left my number," Macie got up the courage to say. "On note."

The confusion left his eyes, and determination took s place. "Where?"

"Where what?"

"Where did you leave the note?"

Macie's head was swirling with confusion. "Right next to ur bed, so you'd see it when you woke up. On the nightstand."

Without a word, Colt grabbed her hand. He turned and p lled her after him as he went up the stairs toward his bedroom. Ma e didn't protest or say anything. She was too weirded out by the wa he was acting.

When they got into his room, he turned to her and said, " how me where."

Macie pointed at the small table next to the bed. The same notepad she'd used that night was still sitting there, along with a pen.

Colt looked at the table, then back at her, then back to the table.

Just when Macie was about to completely wig out, he said, "I didn't see a note from you, Mace. And believe me, I looked. When I woke up and you weren't next to me, I was upset. I had been looking forward to having breakfast with you. To talking with you some more. I got dressed then went downstairs to see if you had left a note there. And once again was disappointed when I didn't find anything. I figured you simply didn't feel the same connection between us that I did."

"I did. I *do*," Macie said. "It was hard for me to leave that note because I was scared you were just being nice. That you didn't mean it when you asked if I wanted to have lunch or something. But I liked you. So I left my number. And you didn't call."

He rubbed his free hand over his face. "God, what a clusterfuck," he muttered. Colt dropped her hand and went over to the bed. He got down on his knees and looked under it. Macie had no idea what he was doing.

Then he reached under the bedframe and pulled out a white sheet of paper and held it up.

She held her breath. The paper had some dust bunnies attached to it, indicating that it had been under his bed for a while.

He hadn't lied. It looked like he really *hadn't* seen her note.

He stood and walked back to her, holding the note between them. She looked down and saw her own handwriting on the small piece of paper.

Colt. Thank you for last night. If you were honest about wanting to have lunch sometime, I'd like that. ~Macie

Her number was clearly written under her short note. Swallowing hard, she looked up at Colt.

"Damn it all to hell," he said softly. "I can't believe I didn't get this. I've wasted so much time."

Macie wasn't sure what to say to that.

"I remember shutting my bedroom door that morning and thinking how glad I was that I didn't live in an apartment when it slammed harder than I'd intended," Colt mused. "I bet it blew off then. All this time, I could've been with you, and I fucked it up."

Now Macie felt bad that he was blaming himself. "I shouldn't have torn it off the pad," she said. "I wasn't thinking straight."

"No," he said immediately, shaking his head. "This isn't your fault. It's mine. I should've manned up and asked Truck for your number anyway. Shit." Colt blew the dust off the note and walked back to the small table. He put the note down, making sure to put the pen on top of it so it didn't get blown off again, then he came back to Macie.

He took both her hands in his and looked down at her. "I would've called that day if I had found the note, Mace. I would've told you then that I had a wonderful night with you, even if it hadn't started under the best circumstances. I would've asked you to lunch. Then after we had lunch, I would've asked you to go with me on a dinner date. I would've asked permission to kiss you at the end of the date, after I'd driven you home. And I would've texted you nonstop after that, and called you when I got home from work, just to hear your voice. I would've bought you silly presents so you wouldn't forget about me. We could've watched movies in your apartment and here at my house. We would've laughed together, and I would've been there for you if you had an anxiety attack. I'm so fucking sorry that I didn't see your note. So sorry."

Macie could feel her heart beating fast in her chest, although this time it wasn't a bad feeling. "We can still do all those things," she got up the courage to say. "It's only been a month and a half since we met."

"I *want* to do those things," Colt said immediately. "And more. But I still hate that we've missed out on a whole month of being together."

Not liking the look of regret on his face, Macie brought her hand up to his neck. Her thumb caressed his chiseled jaw and she said, "Ask permission to kiss me, Colt."

And just like that, the regret faded from his face, to be replaced by hunger. "May I kiss you, Mercedes Laughlin?"

"Yes. Please," she responded.

Macie thought he might crush his lips to hers immediately, but he surprised her by leaning down and placing his lips on her forehead. Then her right cheek, followed by her left. Then he took her hand from the side of his neck and kissed her palm. He dropped it and placed his hands on either side of her neck, his thumbs caressing her jaw like she much as she'd done to him.

"We've somehow managed to screw things up from the get-go, haven't we?" he asked quietly. "But as much as I regret not finding your note and causing you even a second of worry about why I hadn't called you, I love that you're currently living in my house. Sleeping in my bed. In my arms. I haven't pushed for more because the last thing I want to do is rush you—"

"Push me," Macie said, interrupting whatever he was going to say next.

He shook his head. "No. I refuse to rush this. We only have one first kiss. One first time making love. I like this feeling of anticipation. Of knowing that the giddy feeling inside me has returned. It has, hasn't it? You feel it too?"

Macie licked her lips, and loved how his eyes immediately went to her mouth. "Yeah, Colt. I feel it too."

Reverently, he ran a thumb over her lips. Then his beautiful gray eyes met hers and his head lowered.

Macie shut her eyes and waited.

His warm lips brushed hers. Lightly. Achingly soft.

"Heaven," she heard him whisper before his lips were on hers again, this time harder. His tongue brushed against the seam, asking permission to enter. Macie granted him that permission. She opened her mouth and then they were kissing.

Really kissing.

Macie had been kissed before, but nothing compared to how she felt in Colt's arms. His hands kept her head still as he devoured her. She made a noise deep in her throat and gripped Colt's uniform shirt as she took all that he gave her. It was beautiful and carnal at the same time. And the best part was that she didn't feel one inkling of anxiety. Usually when she was with a man, she worried about where she should put her hands, if her breath stunk, if he was enjoying himself…but with Colt, everything else fell to the wayside.

All she could think about was him. And how he made her feel. Nothing else mattered. No one else existed in their little bubble.

Eventually, the kiss gentled. Became less heated. Less desperate. Colt finished their kiss with small pecks and then rested his forehead against hers.

"Wow," Macie said softly.

"Wow, indeed," Colt echoed with a smile.

"You should know something," Macie told him.

He pulled back and took her in, his eyes roaming from her eyes to her mouth, then the slight blush on her cheeks, before returning to her gaze. "Yeah? What's that?"

"There's no way I would've let you kiss me like that a mo th ago," she said honestly. "And as much as I hate that ther was a misunderstanding between us, that kiss made up for it."

He grinned. "It did, didn't it?"

Macie nodded.

"For the record," he added, "I will always remember our irst kiss as one of the most exciting, emotional moments of my life."

"Colt," Macie whispered, feeling overwhelmed. He had a nack for saying the perfect thing at the perfect time.

"Pack," he said, running the back of a hand over her che before stepping away. "I'll change and meet you downstairs. We'll hit he road at soon as you're ready."

She nodded. Suddenly the weekend seemed even more exciting than before. She'd been to Austin, but seeing it with Colt mehow seemed more special.

Macie headed for the door. Even though she'd been stay g in his bed each night, her things were in the guest room, where'd he put her suitcases the first day he'd brought her here.

She looked back right before she exited his room to ee him running a finger over her note on the nightstand.

He looked up and caught her staring. "Things work out e way I hope they do, I'm going to get this framed so it never gets isplaced again."

Macie's throat closed up with happiness and she could 't say a word. She simply smiled at him and turned to go pack.

Chapter Seven

Colt held the hotel door open for Macie and followed her inside. He'd reserved a suite on the river side so they could watch the bats. The day had been fun. He couldn't remember the last time he'd laughed so much. As the commander for two Delta Force teams, he wasn't known for being the most jovial man, but spending time with Macie made him loosen up and simply live in the moment.

They'd arrived Friday night and had ordered room service like they'd planned. Then they'd relaxed and watched a movie on pay-per-view. Macie had fallen asleep halfway through and woke up briefly when he'd gathered her in his arms to sleep.

"I missed the movie," she mumbled.

"Yup. Shhhh, go to sleep," Colt ordered, and she'd immediately closed her eyes and relaxed into him once more.

They'd gotten up early and gone for a walk around the lake. Then they'd had brunch, gone to the antiques store she'd wanted to see and spent several hours there. She'd bought an envelope full of old photos and several more knickknacks. They'd found an eclectic place to eat lunch, then enjoyed the rest of the afternoon wandering around Sixth Street. Colt loved watching her eyes light up when she saw something that interested her. She didn't buy a lot of things, simply enjoyed taking in the ambiance of the quirky stores and shop owners.

They'd arrived back at the hotel in time to watch the bats emerge from under the bridge in search of their nightly meals. Colt laughed at the way Macie squealed and proclaimed she was glad they we e inside behind a window, because there was no way she would en y being anywhere near the animals as they flew off.

Dinner was in the hotel's restaurant, and they were now b: k in the room. They'd been holding hands and touching each other all ay. Colt had even been able to sneak in a few kisses here and there.

The entire day had been building up to this moment, a least in Colt's eyes. It felt like hours of foreplay, which was exciting ra ner than frustrating. He hadn't been this eager to be with a woman for : long as he could remember. He'd dated, but after the incident overseas ne'd lost the desire for any kind of relationship. He concentrated on eing the best commander he could be to protect the men who served un er him.

Until now.

Until Macie.

"Today was awesome," Macie said softly. They were sittii g on the couch in the spacious suite, each drinking a glass of wine.

"Yes it was," Colt agreed. Her hand was resting on his thig n and he covered it with his own.

She stared at him for a long moment before leaning for ard and putting her glass on the coffee table in front of them. Then she took his glass from his hand and placed it next to hers. Colt watched l r take a deep breath before she spoke.

"I haven't been this relaxed in a long time, and it's becau: of you. Usually when I'm in a strange city, I stress about directior ,, who's around me, and what my plans are for the entire day. But I di n't have to do any of that with you. I trusted you to know where you w re going and that you would figure out what we would do all day. It fe good. I like being with you, Colt. I have a question, and I hope you'll l : honest with me."

"Of course I will," Colt answered immediately.

"Does the difference in our ages bother you? Or the fac that I'm Ford's sister? I know he gave you a hard time about the nig t of his wedding. I hadn't told him about it because I thought you saw e as just a friend or something. But now that things are…better betweer us, I got to thinking about the fact that I'm a decade younger than you a ."

"It doesn't bother me in the slightest," Colt told her. " 1 fact, I hadn't even thought about it until you brought it up. Does bother *you?*"

"No," she said immediately. "But I don't want you to get in trouble or have anyone at work say anything because I'm only thirty-three and you're forty-three."

"Listen," Colt said earnestly. "We're both adults. I like you, and you like me. I don't give a flying fuck what other people say about us. And, if you *do* care, I'll do my best to shut that shit down if I hear it. What goes on between us is *only* between us. It's no one else's business. And Truck and I talked. He loves you, Mace. Even though you weren't communicating, he still thought about you and worried about you all these years. I'll admit that he wasn't happy with me, but he's not going to be thrilled about *anyone* being with you, simply because you're his little sister."

"Okay," she said.

"Okay?" he asked.

"Yeah."

"Good."

"So, uh…one more thing," Macie said.

"Anything."

"Will you kiss me again?"

Colt smiled. "Absolutely."

He leaned down and took her lips with his, happy that they were alone and he didn't have to worry about anyone looking at them and saying something that would make Macie uncomfortable—or noticing his hard cock.

He pulled Macie onto his lap so she was straddling him, and set about making sure she knew he was in this one hundred percent. That he didn't care about their ages, or what her brother thought, or anything else that might run through her mind as a roadblock to their relationship.

They'd clicked the night of Truck and Mary's wedding, but when she'd called, scared out of her mind, and he'd been able to help her focus and find a place to hide, something deeper had happened between them. Something on a more primal level.

She was his. His to protect. His to comfort. His to make happy. He hoped down the line she would see him the same way…well, at least as someone she could lean on and rely on. But the soldier in him, the man, wanted her in a way he'd never wanted anyone before.

Before he knew it, Macie was grinding her pussy against his dick, and he was holding her hips, helping her gyrate against him as they kissed. Her hands had shoved his shirt up and were caressing his bare stomach and chest. She wasn't hesitant in any way, and Colt loved that.

He pulled his lips off hers long enough to make sure she was on board with what was happening.

"Are you sure?" He could barely form the words.

"Sure about having sex? Yes! Please."

He grinned at her enthusiastic response and groaned when she leaned forward and nuzzled her nose in the space between his shoulder and neck.

"Birth control?" he ground out, wanting to make sure all their bases were covered before things went too far. He hadn't seen her taking any pills, but that didn't mean she didn't have some other sort of contraceptive.

She froze and sat up. Colt could feel the warmth between her legs, and he fantasized about them doing this again, but with both of them naked.

"I…I'm not on anything," she said after a beat.

"I've got condoms," he reassured her immediately. "I'm clean and haven't been with anyone in over a year, but I'll protect you, Macie. Have no doubt about that."

"I'm clean too," she told him, blushing as she did so. "I didn't sleep with Teddy, so you don't have to worry about that."

"I wasn't worried about it," Colt soothed, even though that was a little white lie. He wasn't concerned for himself so much as he was about her. Teddy obviously wasn't a good man, and anything he'd told her about his sex life had probably been untruthful, so for her sake, he was glad she hadn't gone that far with him.

"It's been, like, four years," Macie blurted. "I just…dating is hard when you have anxiety, and sex seems even harder. So I just stopped doing both. I had my vibrator, so…" She cut herself off with a groan and brought a hand up to her face. "Oh crud. Pretend I didn't say that."

Loving the thought of her pleasuring herself, but not wanting to embarrass her, Colt let that go. "Are you worried about us?" he asked. "Because we can wait. We don't have to do anything other than what we've already done. The last thing I want is to be the source of your anxiety. Ever."

Macie immediately shook her head. "No!" she practically shouted, then her cheeks got even redder. "I mean, no, it's not like that with you. This feels right. Good. I don't want to stop."

"I don't want to stop either," Colt reassured her. "But if at any time you need to slow down or take a break, let me know. I won't be upset and I won't be mad."

"I won't. But okay."

He grinned at her and tightened his hands on her hips again. "Now...where were we?"

"You were about to take me into the other room and make love to me," Macie said with a smile.

And with that, Colt helped Macie off his lap and stood. Then he leaned over and picked her up with an arm behind her back and one under her knees, just like he'd carried her through the parking lot at her apartment complex. He entered the bedroom and put her down on the king-size bed—and just stared at her for a long moment.

"What?"

"You're beautiful," he said reverently.

She shook her head.

"You are," Colt insisted. "Your hair is a beautiful shade of brown that reminds me of a thoroughbred. Your eyes are a deep mahogany that hold so many secrets, they make me want to know every single one. You're the perfect height for me...not too short or too tall."

"I'm too fat."

"No," he countered. "You're perfect. Trust me."

Macie bit her lip and nodded.

Colt could tell she didn't really believe him, but he had plenty of time to make sure she knew he was being one hundred percent honest. For now, he would distract her with pleasure.

He reached down and pulled his shirt up and over his head, loving how Macie's eyes didn't leave his body. Wanting to make her feel comfortable, he undid the button and zipper on his jeans and slowly shoved them down his legs. His socks came off next, and then he was standing in front of her with nothing on but his underwear. Briefs that in no way hid his desire for her. He could feel his dick pulsing with desire for the woman in front of him.

"Your turn," he said quietly, not making a move toward her.

Macie looked up at him and, without breaking eye contact, undid the buttons of her light blue blouse one by one. He looked down when she shook off her shirt and stared at the beauty she'd unveiled f r him.

Her tits were still encased in her bra, but his mouth actically watered with the need to suck on them. The bra was a lacy ing that showcased her chest rather than hiding it. With every heaving b eath she took, her tits looked as if they were going to pop right out and pill over the cups.

Colt watched as her hands quickly unbuttoned her jeans and she lifted her hips to push them down. She kicked them off, and e barely noticed when they landed in a heap on the floor next to the be He was mesmerized by the sight of her.

Her legs seemed to be miles long, but he couldn't take his es away from the slight scrap of lace between her thighs. He could actically smell her arousal, and it increased his own tenfold.

He took a step toward the bed and thanked his lucky star that she was his. And not just for tonight, if he had anything to say abc t it. She was *his*. Forever.

Slowly, he put a knee on the mattress next to her, and sl smiled even as she scooted over to give him room on the giant matt ss. Colt didn't hesitate; he moved one knee over her body until he was raddling her and lowered himself. He put his weight on his elbows and ighed in ecstasy as they touched from hips to chest. His cock was hard between her legs, but he wouldn't hide his reaction from her.

"Hey," he said when they were face to face.

"Hey," she returned with a small smile.

He felt her hands move up his sides then rest on his naked ack.

"You ready for this? For us?"

"I feel as if I've been waiting for this my entire life."

It was the perfect answer. Colt smiled and kissed her. T y made out for several minutes, lazy, long sweeps of the tongue, pl ful and easy. Then the kiss changed. Became more urgent. He felt l r hands clutch his back as her hips arched up into him.

He drew back from her mouth and moved down her bod He put his fingertips on the edge of the cups of her bra and looked p. "May I?"

Macie nodded eagerly.

Slowly and carefully, Colt pulled down her bra until her tit popped out. He inhaled deeply at the sight of her erect little nipples. She was plenty bountiful in the chest department, and something abo t seeing how turned on she was flicked a switch inside him.

He couldn't be gentle anymore.

He'd been trying so hard to be a considerate and easy lover so he didn't scare her in any way, but the second he saw the evidence of her arousal, he lost it.

His mouth descended on one nipple as if it held the elixir of life. Colt didn't lick and tease, either—he sucked her nipple hard, pushing it up to the roof of his mouth with his tongue as he did so. Reaching for her other nipple, he pinched it with his fingers, making it even harder.

She wiggled under him, arched her back to press deeper, and groaned. Loving how responsive she was, Colt continued his assault on her breasts. He couldn't get enough. He pushed them together and switched off, sucking on one nipple then the other.

"Take it off," he mumbled even as he devoured her.

"What?" she asked, dazed.

"Your bra. Take it off," he ordered.

"Oh!"

And with that, she arched her back even more—which Colt took advantage of—and reached under herself to unhook the contraption.

The second she was free, he palmed both breasts and squeezed. "Fuck, woman. Beautiful." Colt knew he wasn't speaking in full sentences, but that was beyond him at the moment.

It took several seconds for him to realize that Macie was attempting to push his underwear down his legs. He wanted to stop her. To tell her that he was on a hair trigger and if he took them off, he'd blow.

But then she looked up at him, her pupils dilated with lust, and said, "I want you inside me."

That did it. He couldn't deny her anything. He was a dead man. If she ever realized the power she held over him, he'd be in big trouble.

Colt rolled onto his back and shoved his underwear down his thighs, wincing as his cock sprang free in the process. He felt movement next to him and looked over at Macie. She'd done the same thing, and now lay naked as the day she was born next to him, smiling.

As quick as a flash, Colt resumed his position over her, this time his cock brushing against the curls between her legs.

"Fuck me," she repeated, lifting her hips in invitation.

Knowing he had no control, and wanting to make sure Macie was slick and ready for him, Colt eased himself down her body, kissing his way from her chest, to her tits, to her belly button and beyond.

Macie tugged at him. "Colt. Please!"

"I'm going to fuck you, Macie. Make no mistake. But first, I'm going to taste you. I'm going to make you come with my mouth and fingers. Then when you're exhausted and sated, I'm going to put my cock inside you and make love to you. You won't know where you end and I begin…and I'm going to make you come again. *Then*, when you're incoherent with pleasure, I'm going to fuck you. That work for you?"

Colt didn't know where the words were coming from. He'd never been a dirty talker. Preferred to just get down to business and get off. But he wanted to cherish every second of this first time with Macie. Wanted her to be as mindless with pleasure as he knew *he* would be.

"Uh…yeah, Colt. That works for me. I'll just lie here and let you…you know…do your thing."

"Thank you," he said with a smile. Fuck, she was adorable. Then he bent his head and did his thing.

* * * *

Macie shook as the orgasm tore through her. Colt had done exactly what he'd said he was going to do. He'd put his mouth on her and made her come. Oh, his fingers had been involved too, but mostly it was the way his tongue curled around her clit and the way he'd sucked the sensitive bundle of nerves that had thrown her over the edge.

She'd never really enjoyed oral sex, because she always worried about what she smelled like, what she tasted like, and if the guy was going to want her to reciprocate. But with Colt, she couldn't think about anything but how good he was making her feel.

And for the first time ever, she wanted to return the favor. She *wanted* to get her mouth on his cock. She'd caught a glimpse of his dick when he'd removed his underwear, and it was quite impressive.

Before she could reach for him, or let him know she wanted to touch him too, he was looming over her once more. She loved the feel of him on top of her. She felt surrounded by him, and it made her feel safe. Loved.

He knelt up and reached over to the table next to the bed and grabbed a condom. She watched him roll it down his length with greedy eyes. She'd been right. He *was* impressive. She must've made a noise in her throat, because his gaze came back to her, and he smiled.

"You want this?" he asked.

"Yes," she said bluntly.

He took hold of his dick with one hand and inched his knees up, spreading her legs wider. Macie looked down and saw the mushroom head of his cock pressing against her folds. She lifted her hips, welcoming him into her heat.

The sound of his groan as he slowly pressed into her hot, wet body was almost as satisfying as the feel of him inside her. Almost.

Closing her eyes at the sensation, Macie arched her spine and threw back her head. She gripped his biceps and sucked in a breath through her nose. He was big, and it had been a long time since she'd had a man.

As if he understood, Colt held completely still inside her, letting her get used to him. She heard him murmuring comforting words as her body relaxed.

"Better?" he asked softly.

Macie nodded.

He pulled out of her body all the way, then slowly pressed inside again, piercing her folds once more. Then he did it again. And again.

She'd never been made love to this way. In the past, the men had just hammered inside of her until they'd come.

But every time Colt pulled away, her hips followed, not wanting to lose him. Then he'd press his cock back inside and she'd feel whole again.

Reaching down, she gripped his ass and dug her nails into his sensitive skin when he left her body once more. "Colt," she griped.

"What?" he asked with a grin.

"Stay inside me," she ordered.

"You're more sensitive this way though, aren't you?" he asked.

Thinking about it, Macie nodded. "Yeah. All the nerve endings down there come to life every time you pull all the way out before pushing back in."

"Exactly," he muttered. "For me too. My cock is all happy and warm, then it's cold and sad, then it's happy and warm again."

Macie chuckled and Colt groaned. "Fuck, I can feel your muscles clenching around my dick when you laugh."

That made her laugh harder, and she wrapped her legs around his thighs, trying to hold him in place. "I thought you said you were going to make me come slow and easy?" she complained.

"You ready for that?" he asked. "I was giving you time to recover."

"I'm recovered," she reassured him.

Instead of picking up his pace, Colt pressed all the way inside her, then sat up, pulling her ass onto his thighs. Her pelvis was tilted upward and she was resting on her shoulder blades. She was about to ask what he was doing—when his thumb landed on her clit and began stroking, slow and easy.

Squirming, wanting more but somehow less, Macie gasped. "What are you doing?"

"Making love to you. Making you come on my cock."

The movement of his thumb was relentless. No matter how much she squirmed, she couldn't get away from it. His cock was full and hard inside her, and her body bore down on it as she got closer and closer to losing it.

"Damn, hon. You're squeezing me *so* hard. It feels so fucking good. You need to come or I'll lose it."

She barely heard his words. Macie had always thought she needed a fast and hard touch on her clit to come, but Colt was proving her wrong. The orgasm built slowly but steadily until Macie knew she was about to tumble over. She spread her legs as wide as she could as her thighs began to tremble. Her stomach clenched and her toes curled.

"That's it, Mace. Come for me."

And she did.

She thought she might've blacked out for a moment because when she became aware of where she was again, her ass was back on the mattress and Colt was leaning over her once more. He was still inside her, as hard as ever.

"I'm going to fuck you now," he said roughly. "*Hard*. You ready?"

Macie nodded. She was ready for whatever he wanted to do with her. She was his. Completely.

His hips started moving, pressing his length in and out of her. Sweat beaded on his brow as he fought his body's reaction. I'm not going to last," he informed her. "Watching you come, hearing my name on your lips, feeling your excitement on my thighs…it was too much. Does this feel okay?"

Macie nodded.

"Touch yourself," he ordered. "Make yourself come again."

"I can't," she protested, even as her hips rose to meet his thrusts.

"Try," he croaked. "*Please*. I want to feel you squeeze the come out of me."

Not able to deny him anything, Macie reached down between their bodies and brushed a finger over her swollen clit. She jerked in response. She was so sensitive still. Even though it hurt a little bit, she did as Colt asked. She wanted to please him. Wanted to force him over the edge with her.

It didn't take long. Within a minute Macie felt the telltale signs of her impending orgasm. "I'm close!" she warned.

"I know," he responded. "Do it! Fucking come."

It took another ten seconds or so, but she did. Just moments after she began trembling and shaking from the intense bliss, Colt threw his head back and shuddered. The muscles in his arms next to her shook with the pleasure he was experiencing and his chest heaved with his breaths. It was awe inspiring and hot as hell.

As if a plug had been pulled, Colt relaxed. He dropped down and rolled, taking Macie with him. She lay on top of him now, his dick slowly softening inside her. They didn't say anything for the longest time, not until he slid out of her.

Macie whimpered a protest; she'd liked how he'd felt. How they were connected.

"I know," he whispered. "I liked being in there too."

Macie knew he had to get up and take care of the condom. It had to be uncomfortable, now that they were done, but he didn't make any move to leave the bed.

"Every morning, I wake up in a momentary panic, thinking you'll have left in the middle of the night," Colt admitted softly.

Macie felt awful about that. "I'm sorry."

"Don't be. Just promise that you'll never again leave my bed without telling me. If you have to get up and pee in the middle of the night, fine, but if you can't sleep and are going to go read or work, wake me up and let me know. I can't handle waking up to you being gone, Mace. Not after tonight."

"I promise." It was an easy promise to make.

"I'll do the same. It's much more likely that I'll be the one leaving," he said. "We get called to the base in the middle of the night for missions sometimes, and I always need to go in and monitor my men, but I'll never leave without saying goodbye. That's my vow to you."

"Thank you." Macie couldn't say anything else through the lump in her throat.

Then Colt rolled them over once more and kissed her. It was a long, lazy kiss that felt comfortable and easy. She was exhausted from three orgasms and was on the verge of falling asleep when he pulled away.

He smiled down at her, then kissed her on the forehead. "Sleep, hon. I'll be right back after I take care of this condom."

Macie watched as Colt climbed out of the bed and walked butt-naked to the bathroom. He didn't seem the least concerned that he wasn't wearing any clothes. But why would he? For a forty-three-year-old man, he was in excellent shape. He didn't exactly have a six-pack anymore, but his muscles were clearly defined and his ass was to die for.

Smiling to herself, Macie closed her eyes. She soon felt the mattress depress, and Colt gathered her into his arms. He covered them with a blanket and kissed her temple. That was the last thing Macie remembered before falling into one of the best sleeps she'd had in a very long time.

Chapter Eight

"So you're telling us that you can't find her ex, and you can't track down the men he associates with, who were most likely the ones who broke into her apartment not once, but twice?"

Macie winced at the censure in Colt's tone. They'd driven to Lampasas to grab some more clothes from her apartment and had stopped at the police station to talk to the detective.

"It's not as easy as the shows on television make it look," the man tried to defend himself.

Colt and the detective went into stare-down mode, and Macie shifted uncomfortably. She hated being the cause of this conflict. She didn't really know the detective, but he'd been trying to find Teddy for almost a month.

It was hard to believe an entire month had passed since she'd called her brother needing help. One month since she'd moved in with Colt. The happiest month of her life.

Oh, there were plenty of times when her anxiety overwhelmed her, but somehow, with Colt by her side, things seemed easier. Less stressful. When she went to the grocery store, she worried less if people were staring at her. She went out to eat more because she could sit next to Colt, and if there was something wrong with the food or the service, he dealt with it. And when she'd had a major anxiety attack after one of her clients hated the website she'd spent days designing, Colt had been there to rub her back and reassure her that her entire career wasn't over.

It was nice having someone in her corner.

No, it was more than nice. It was a miracle.

And Macie was scared to death, every day, that she would o or say something to screw things up between them, and then she'd e alone once more. She'd have to move back to her apartment here in mpasas and worry that the men who'd broken in hadn't been caught yet

After staring at the detective for a full minute, Colt fir lly said, "You have my contact information if you find them."

"I'll be in touch with Mercedes, as it's her case," the dete ive said firmly.

Macie saw Colt's jaw tighten.

She *hated* confrontation. It was one of the things that co ld easily throw her into a full-blown anxiety attack. "Thank you," she blurted, tugging on Colt's arm. "I would appreciate that. I'm sure you e doing everything you can to find them."

Colt's mouth opened as if he wanted to say something, ut after looking at her, he obviously changed his mind. He nodde at the detective, wrapped an arm around her waist and steered her to vard the exit.

The second they were out of earshot of the detective, leaned down and asked, "You okay?"

Macie nodded. She could feel her heart beating way too ast, but she took a few deep breaths to try to control it.

Colt held open the door for her, and his palm at the sm l of her back felt nice. Comforting. His touch reminded her of how the 'd made love the night before. She'd been on her knees in his bed and h 'd taken her from behind. His hand had caressed the small of her back, ist as he was doing now.

Just the thought of Colt making love to her was enoug to help snap Macie out of her downward spiral. He was an amazingly enerous lover, always making sure she got just as much pleasure ou of their joining as he did.

After Colt had gotten her settled in his Wrangler and clin ed into the driver's side, he turned to look at her. "I'm going to see vhat my team can do to find this guy."

Macie blinked. She'd been lost in her thoughts about Colt and her, naked in bed together, and his mind was obviously in a c mpletely different place than hers.

"You're going to get Ford and his friends involved?" She wasn't sure she wanted that. Macie had no doubt her brother could probably track down Teddy, but she wasn't sure he'd be able to keep his shit together long enough to find out any information from him. Ford was *pissed*. Extremely pissed that Teddy had obviously targeted her as an easy mark. As someone he could use to hide his drugs, or whatever it was he'd stashed in her apartment.

"No, not Truck. He'd lose his shit and do something stupid, which could hurt his career. I'm talking about the other Delta team I command."

Macie nodded in understanding. She hadn't met the men he was referring to, but she knew of them.

"Because Trigger and his crew don't have any connection to you, it will be easier for them to look into this. I'll talk to him tonight. Ask him to have Brain see what he can find."

"Why Brain?" Macie asked.

"Because Brain is a sneaky son of a bitch and is smarter than anyone I've ever met in my life. The man could have been a brain surgeon or a nuclear physicist, but he chose to enlist in the Army instead. He'll be able to use technology the cops don't have to see if Teddy is even still in the area, and then the others can use his intel to track him down."

Macie bit her lip and stared at Colt.

"What?" he asked, reaching out and caressing her lip with his thumb.

"I...I don't want anyone to get in trouble. Least of all you and your men. Maybe, if no one has been back to my apartment since that second break-in and the detective can't find Teddy, he left town."

"Maybe," Colt agreed. "But I'm not taking the chance that he isn't just lying low, waiting for the perfect time to strike against you. We still don't know what it was he was looking for. Maybe those thugs *did* find whatever it was when they searched your apartment that second time, but we don't know for sure. And until I'm one hundred percent certain you're safe, I'm not taking any chances."

Macie's chest felt tight, but this time it wasn't because she was on the verge of panicking. No one in her entire life had ever gone to as much trouble to look after her as Colt. Sure, Ford had done his best to take care of her when they were kids, but this was different. And strangely enough, knowing what Colt had done to get to his friend Gris, how violently he'd defended him, made her feel confident in his ability to keep her safe.

"Maybe we should go back to my apartment and look through everything again?" Macie suggested.

Colt shook his head. "No. Not today. You've had enough, and if we didn't find anything the first time we looked, then we probably won't find anything the second time."

"Do you think Teddy knows where I've been staying?" Macie asked quietly. She'd been worried about it for a while, which was why she was more than content to stay in the house when Colt went to work every day. He had a security system, and it was easier on her psyche.

Colt looked at her for a long moment before finally nodding. "Yeah, hon. I think it's possible. If he's smart—and I think he is, because he's managed to elude the cops for this long—he probably had someone watching your apartment, and when Truck and the others showed up to get more of your stuff or to check things out, he could've had them follow us back to Killeen."

Macie bit her lip again. Then asked, "Am I putting you in danger?"

With that, Colt leaned over and put his hand on the back of her neck and pulled her closer to him. Macie braced her hand on the console between them but didn't try to pull away from him. "I can handle that punk Teddy. Brain got his rap sheet for me, and believe me, he doesn't scare me."

"But—"

"No buts," Colt said firmly, interrupting her before she could even start to protest. He kissed her briefly, then pulled back to look her in the eyes. "I like having you in my house. In my bed. I like seeing your computer and files on my dining room table. I just plain like you, Macie. This isn't a hardship for me. If I had my way, you'd stay even after this is over. So if you think I'm gonna let a punk like Theodore Dorentes hurt you, you're crazy."

She liked everything he'd just said, but one thing stood out. "You want me to stay?"

"Yeah, Mace. I want you to stay," he confirmed.

She *should* tell him he was insane. That she had way too many issues to be a good bet. That he'd helped her feel more normal recently, but her anxiety would always be an issue. That as a colonel, he needed a partner who was outgoing and social, which would never be her. That she always second-guessed people's motives for doing anything.

But she kept quiet. She wanted Colt more than she'd ever wanted anything in her life, and if he didn't understand how fucked-up she was, then she wasn't going to tell him.

"I like you just the way you are," he added after a moment, as if he could see what she was thinking. "There will always be people who misunderstand us, but as long as we're good with who we are together, then fuck them."

She wished she was as confident as Colt, but she gave him a small nod anyway. He leaned forward and kissed her again. "You ready to go home?"

Home. Yeah, she could totally get used to that. "Yes," she said simply.

Even though it had been a weird day, and Macie should be stuck in her head and dealing with her insecurities, she wasn't. She smiled all the way back to Killeen.

* * * *

Colt sat in his office with his hands steepled under his chin as he looked across the desk at the seven men on the second Delta Force team he commanded. He'd asked to speak to Trigger, and told him why, and the next thing he knew, the entire team was there.

"All due respect," Grover had told him, "but if someone is threatening our commander's woman, it's *all* of our concern, not just Trigger's."

Colt couldn't get upset with the men for that. Besides, the more people he had looking out for Macie, the better, in his opinion. So he'd outlined what had happened at her apartment complex and who Teddy was. He explained that Macie was staying at his house, and hopefully would be moving in with him permanently, if he could convince her. He told his men about the Lampasas police not being able to find Teddy or the men who'd broken into Macie's apartment, and he finally touched on the anxiety that Macie fought on a daily basis.

Like the good men he knew they were, not one of the guys in front of him looked discomfited with that last revelation. In fact, Trigger asked, "That's what happened at the reception, isn't it?"

"Yeah," Colt said.

Lefty nodded. "Brain noticed that she didn't look well and was going to deal with it when you beat him to it."

Colt turned his attention to Brain and eyed the younger man.

Brain smiled and held up his hands in a conciliatory gesture. "I knew she was Truck's sister and just wanted to make sure she was okay. That's all."

Colt nodded and tried to calm down. Brain wasn't going to hit on Macie. He was being polite, that's all.

"Yeah," he said, answering Trigger's question. "The wedding and reception were hard for her. Social situations generally are, so I took her home and made sure she was all right."

The men all nodded. "So what's the plan?" Oz asked.

"Brain, I'd like you to see what you can do to find Teddy. Figure out where he likes to hang out, who his dealer is, and who his friends are.

"Doc and Grover, if you can watch her apartment when you can, and see if you notice anyone lurking around, I'd appreciate it. We don't know who the assholes were who broke in and threatened Macie, and I don't like that they're still out there somewhere. Lucky and Oz, I'd appreciate you doing surveillance of my neighborhood. There's no evidence that Teddy or his friends have been to Killeen, but I don't want to take any chances. We don't know what it was that Teddy was looking for, so he might decide to try to get to Macie directly."

"And us, sir?" Trigger asked, referring to himself and Lefty.

"I want you to come over after we leave here and let me introduce you to her."

"Sir?" Lefty asked.

"I told you that she suffers from anxiety. She eventually needs to meet all of you. Needs to get comfortable with you. She's already comfortable with Truck and his team, mostly because of the fact he's her brother. But I want her to get to know all of you, as well. If I have my way, she's going to be around for a hell of a long time, and the last thing I want is for her to feel anxious about seeing any of you. I'm going to need your help in social situations to keep her calm. I won't be able to be by her side at all times, and if she knows you reprobates, then we can both relax."

"Done," Trigger said immediately.

"It's not like I have plans," Lefty added. "I'd love to get to know her."

"What about the rest of us?" Grover smirked. "I want to meet the woman who has our commander wrapped around her finger."

Colt stood and leaned over his desk and glared at his soldier. "Damn straight, she does," he said in a low tone. "And I'll do whatever it takes to protect her. Remember that, soldier."

Grover immediately nodded. "Of course, sir. I didn't mean anything by that."

Colt tried to get his temper under control. He knew Grover didn't mean to be disrespectful, but his comment still rubbed him the wrong way. "She's smart as all get out," he told his men. "Beautiful. Resourceful. And she's been through hell in her life. She's sensitive about the things people say. She assumes they're talking about her, even if they aren't. Watch what comes out of your mouth, and be respectful at all times. Got it?"

A chorus of "Yes, sir" rang out in the room.

"Good," Colt said with a nod. "If you have any concerns, anything at all, you call me first and the cops second. I don't expect you to protect her with your life, that's going a bit far, but I do expect that you'll look after her as you would each others' women."

"Sir," Trigger said, "you don't need to tell us that. We may not have wives like everyone on Ghost's team does, but that doesn't mean we don't respect their women, and even want our own at some point. It's obvious that Macie is important to you, and therefore she's important to us too. She's as much a part of this team as you are. You can count on us to do whatever it takes to make sure she's safe."

Colt relaxed even further. He hadn't realized he wanted and needed their support so much. "Thank you. Dismissed."

The team headed out of his office and Colt took a deep breath.

He had a bad feeling about the entire situation. Too much time had passed since Macie's apartment had been broken into. Men like her ex didn't have a lot of patience...so why hadn't he made a move before now? Every day that went by was another day that his anger could fester and grow. The situation made Colt uneasy, and if he could, he would bring Macie to work with him every day, just to make sure she was safe.

The only thing making him not lose his mind was the knowledge that Macie wasn't the kind of woman to take risks. That was one of the one million and two things he loved about her. He dealt with enough risks and danger at his job. Knowing she had no intentions of leaving his house when he was at work made him feel better about the situation.

He hadn't ordered her not to. Hadn't told her of his suspicions about her ex. She'd actually brought it up one night when they were lying in bed together, replete and relaxed after making love. She'd told him that she felt safer holed up in his house when he was at work because Teddy still hadn't been found. She volunteered to stay safely behind his locked doors during the day and only leave when he was with her.

He hated that she felt that way, but he hadn't argued with her. Hopefully, after they figured out where Teddy was and he was dealt with, he could work with her on feeling more confident about going out on her own.

Taking a deep breath, Colonel Robinson got back to work.

* * * *

Later that night, after he'd reassured himself that Macie was doing well, he told her that Trigger and Lefty would be stopping by. She looked unsure, but nodded.

"These are my men," Colt told her. "Do you think I'd let them into your life if I thought they would do or say anything that would cause you one iota of mental anguish?"

"Well, no, but...that doesn't mean I'm not nervous about meeting them."

"Hon, every single one of my men would do exactly what I did all those years ago if something were to happen to me. If I was captured by the Taliban, I know with a bone-deep conviction that they'd move heaven and Earth to free me...just as I'd do for them. But it's more than that. Just as your brother would do whatever it takes to keep you safe, I'd do the same for him. And for Mary. And for Ghost and Rayne, or Casey and Beatle...or any of them and their wives and children. The bond we have goes deeper than simply soldier and commander. It's because of what we do. How we rely on each other to have our backs in the most intense situations of our lives."

They were standing by the kitchen, and Colt reached out and pulled Macie into his embrace until they were touching from thighs to chest.

One hand spanned her lower back and the other buried itself in the hair at her neck. He rested his forehead against hers and continued. "I love you, Macie. It's scary how much. Now that I've experienced life with you, I don't want it any other way. Now that I know how it feels to come home from work to you, I never want to come home to an empty house again. Now that I've been lucky enough to hold you in my arms every night for over a month, I can't go without it. And now that I've been inside you, felt you come on my cock, I can't imagine being intimate with another woman for as long as I live. You're *it* for me. I'm putty in your hands. My men know that—and they'll do whatever it takes to protect you because you're a part of me."

By this time, Macie was crying. She wasn't making a sound, but tears coursed down her cheeks.

"You do *not* have to be nervous about meeting Trigger or Lefty. Or Oz, Doc, Brain, Grover, or Lucky. They will treat you with respect. They will love you. They will be your brothers in every way that matters. They'll have your back and your side and your front. You can trust them to be there for you when you need them, no matter what that means. Eventually, when they find them, their women will be your friends too. I don't know what's in store for them, who they'll find to complete them, but I know those women are out there, waiting. And they'll love you just as much as I do. Want to know how I know that?"

She didn't answer verbally, but looked up at him with her beautiful brown eyes filled with tears and nodded.

"Because you're you," Colt said. "You're considerate, kind, compassionate, down-to-earth, and so damn likable it's hard for me to understand how you don't see it yourself."

"I love you too," she said softly, and Colt closed his eyes, overwhelmed with emotion. He knew how hard it was for her to say the words, and he swore right then and there to never take them for granted.

He opened his eyes again. "I'm the luckiest man in the world," he told her before using his thumbs to wipe away the tears on her cheeks. Then he leaned down and kissed her. It was a slow kiss that started out tender and sweet, but by the time he pulled back, his cock was hard and she was pressing herself into him eagerly.

"As much as I'd like to lift you onto the counter, pull down your jeans and bury my face in your delectable pussy, I don't have time.

100/*Susan Stoker*

Trigger and Lefty will be here any minute."

"Rain check?" she asked with a small smile.

Colt grinned. "Fuck yeah. You want to go freshen up before they get here?"

She nodded, but didn't pull away from him. "Colt?"

"Yeah, hon?"

"I can't imagine my life without you in it either."

He couldn't stop himself from kissing her once more. After several moments, he forced himself to stop touching her, and he took a step back. "Upstairs with you, woman."

She giggled at him and nodded, turning and heading for the stairs.

Colt watched her every step of the way. He stood where he was long after she'd disappeared from view, wondering how in the world he'd gotten so lucky.

Chapter Nine

A week later, Macie sat at Colt's dining room table, working on her laptop. Over the last seven days, she'd not only met Trigger and Lefty, but the other men on Colt's second Delta Force team as well.

They reminded her of her brother in a lot of ways. They were funny and polite, but there was an edge to them that was a reminder they were also lethal.

Most of the men were around her age. They varied in height and physical characteristics, but every single one had an intense look that would have made her nervous if Colt hadn't been by her side. But by the time they'd left the house after their visits, she'd felt comfortable with each and every one of them. She could totally understand Colt's devotion to them, and the devotion they had to their commanding officer in return.

It was weird for Macie to think about Colt as a commander. To her, he was just Colt, but it was obvious that he garnered a great deal of respect from his men.

Hearing a noise from her computer that meant she had a new email, Macie opened the program and read over the panicked email from one of her former clients. Somehow, her website had reverted to data that had been on it two years ago and everything was now out of date.

"Shit," Macie muttered, and got to work trying to figure out what the issue was. After thirty minutes, she sat back in defeat. There had been an update to the platform the author was using, but no one had backed up the data on her website since Macie had done the work two years ago. Macie was pretty sure she could fix it, but the coding she'd done in the past was on an older backup drive at her apartment in Lampasas.

She fired off a note to the author, telling her that she was willing to work on the emergency issue and spelling out how much it would cost. Macie might not be good at face-to-face interactions with people, always worrying over what they thought or were saying about her, but one thing she'd learned over the years was that she couldn't beat around the bush when it came to money.

Her clients appreciated knowing upfront how much she charged, and Macie appreciated being paid in a timely manner.

The author immediately emailed back, accepting the price for Macie's help, but insisted that it had to be done as soon as possible. She couldn't wait because she had a new book coming out in a couple days. It was book three in a new series, and as the website stood now, the other two books in the series weren't on there. She had to have her site fixed.

It was a small disaster, and Macie couldn't blame the author for being frantic. She bit her thumbnail and considered her options. She could recode the website from scratch, but that would take forever and would cost the author considerably more. If she could get the work she'd already done from her apartment, there was a chance she could have the website fixed and up and running by tonight.

But the *last* thing she was going to do was drive over to Lampasas on her own. She wasn't an idiot. Not when neither Colt and his teams nor the police had found Teddy yet.

Macie felt her chest get tight as she thought through what she should do. She could tell the author she simply had to wait, but that wouldn't be good for her reputation. The author might turn around and bad-mouth her to others, and she could be blackballed in the profession. Macie knew Colt was busy today. He'd told her that he had meetings with other high-ranking officers on the Army post. They were setting up a new mission for Ford and his team, and the last thing Macie wanted to do was ask Colt to drop that for something that wasn't an emergency.

Well, it was an emergency for the author, but she didn't think that really counted when compared to making sure her brother was safe when he was sent out of the country on a top-secret mission.

Macie thought about Trigger and the others on his team. Trigger had made sure she understood that she could contact him at any time, and had added his contact information to her phone.

Biting her lip, Macie decided to wait for Colt to get home. He'd go with her to her apartment and get the drive she needed. She could just stay up late tonight, updating the website. It wouldn't be the first time she'd lost sleep because of work.

But then another email popped up from the author. She had a newsletter that was supposed to go out that evening, and it had a link to her website for people to preorder the new book, *and* her public relations woman was on vacation and couldn't update the email before it went out to literally tens of thousands of readers.

The pressure built in Macie's chest. She had to have that code today. As soon as possible.

Without thinking too hard about what she was doing, Macie picked up her phone and clicked on Trigger's name.

"Hello?"

"Hi. Uh...Trigger?"

"Macie? What's wrong? Are you all right? Where are you?"

"I'm fine," she reassured him quickly. "I'm at home...er...Colt's house. I...uh...something came up, and I know Colt is busy. Ford too. I wouldn't ask, but it's important." The words were stilted, but Macie was proud that she'd gotten them out at all.

"You're okay? You're not hurt?" Trigger asked.

"No. I'm fine." She heard him sigh in relief.

"Okay. So what's up? What can I do to help?"

"If you can't, I totally understand. I mean, you're probably at work and it's not like you can just leave whenever you want. Isn't that called going AWOL? Absent without leave? I don't want you to get in trouble—"

"Macie. What do you need?" Trigger asked, a hint of exasperation in his tone.

Macie closed her eyes and blurted it out. "I need something from my apartment. I don't want to go by myself, and Colt and Ford are busy. It won't take but two seconds for me to run in and grab it."

"What do you need? Can I pick something up for you on my way to Colt's house?" Trigger asked.

It was a nice thought, but unfortunately unhelpful. She quickly explained the situation, and finished with, "It'll save me hours of work and my client hundreds of dollars if I can get the drive and use what I've already done."

Trigger was quiet for so long, Macie wasn't sure he was still there. "Trigger?"

"I don't suppose you'll let me drive to Lampasas and pick it up for you?" he asked.

Macie sighed. "I would, but I honestly don't know where the drive is. I know I put a bunch of stuff in my front closet, but with the police being there and looking through things to try to find what had been disturbed, plus those men rifling through everything, it could be anywhere by now. I'm not sure you'd be able to find it, especially when I don't remember exactly where it should be in the first place."

"I'm on my way. Do *not* leave the house before I get there," Trigger ordered.

"Of course not."

"I'll be there in ten minutes or less." And with that, he hung up.

Macie sighed and clicked off her phone. She wasn't happy about needing to go to her apartment. The place gave her the creeps now, but she did need her old files.

Macie pushed back from the table and stood—then stilled as something occurred to her.

If she moved in with Colt permanently, she wouldn't have to worry about needing things that might still be at her apartment.

The second the thought crossed her mind, she realized just how much she wanted that.

Things between her and Colt had happened fast, but she couldn't deny there had been something between them at her brother's wedding. There was no way she would've stayed the night with him if she hadn't felt it. And she never would've gotten up the courage to leave him her number either. It didn't matter that he hadn't seen it; the fact that the spark had still been there a month later was enough for Macie to realize he was different from any man she'd met thus far.

Then her shoulders slumped.

She'd never bring it up with him. No way. She wasn't brave enough. She'd never force herself on him. She fought a constant war in her head that things weren't the way she imagined they were. And it would kill her if she brought up moving all her things into his house and Colt vetoed the idea.

Taking a deep breath, Macie did her best to stop her line of thinking before it went any further. She knew she wasn't the best bet when it came to a partner. She'd take more than she'd give. But Colt had said he loved her, and she'd said it back, and the Earth hadn't stopped moving.

She ran upstairs and changed into a pair of jeans and put on a bra before going back downstairs and tidying up her work area. Just when she was about to go crazy from waiting, she heard a knock. Checking the peephole and seeing it was Trigger, she opened the door. "I'm ready," she told him.

Trigger was good-looking. As far as she could tell he was a couple years older than her and even taller than Colt. He had dark hair and an intense look in his eyes that Macie figured someone would take one look at and back off. But, because of Colt's little speech the other night, Macie wasn't afraid of him. She wasn't particularly worried about what he thought of her either, mostly because of Colt, but also due to how friendly and open Trigger had been when she'd first met him.

"The faster we go, the faster we can get back," Trigger said.

Macie eyed him and asked, "Do you think it's too dangerous? I'll wait for Colt if you think it'll be safer. The last thing I want is to put you in danger."

"I can handle your ex," Trigger said with a hint of disgust in his voice. "And I didn't mean anything by that statement. I just know you're more comfortable here than in your own place. And it's hot as hell out here today."

Macie smiled. Texas always seemed to be hot, but today was oppressive even by Texas standards.

She set the alarm by punching the code into the box on the wall then shut and locked the door. She followed Trigger to his vehicle, a sleek black Porsche, and smiled when he opened her side of the car for her. When they were on their way, she asked about the sleek sports car.

Trigger shrugged a little self-consciously. "I'm single and have saved up a lot of money. Why not?"

"I like it," Macie reassured him. "Have you guys found out anything else about Teddy or who he had break in?"

Trigger sighed and ran a hand through his hair. "Not as much as we want. Brain has tracked down a few leads, and we've passed them on to the detective in charge of your case, but either Teddy is the luckiest son of a bitch alive, or he's gotten help from someone we've missed.'

"I think it's probably the latter. I mean, I'm not that confident with people, but something about him made me put down my guard faster than I normally would. I have a feeling he's conned a lot of people."

"I know you're right," Trigger said. "And you shouldn't feel bad about dating him. Some people just have more charisma than others, and if he chose to use it to be an asshole, that's on him, not you."

Macie nodded, not completely convinced. The rest of the trip, she worried about why Teddy had singled her out. Did she look that gullible? She tried to remember when she'd first seen him in person, and couldn't. That said a lot about how she really felt about him.

She could remember the first time she saw Colt. It was in Ford's hospital room after he'd been injured at the holdup at Mary's bank. She'd felt the chemistry between them then, but it was at Ford's wedding when she really took notice of him. He was sitting near the front of the church in his dress blue Army uniform. He had a half smile on his face the entire time.

Macie remembered thinking that he looked like a man a woman could count on.

And she hadn't been wrong.

"We're here," Trigger said, snapping her out of the mini trance she'd been in. "I'm going to come around and open your door for you."

Macie nodded and watched as he unfolded himself from the low-slung sports car and strode around the front of the vehicle. He held out a hand to help her out and stayed right by her side as they walked up the stairs to her apartment.

It was the first time she'd been back in a few weeks. The apartment smelled a bit musty. Wrinkling her nose, she turned to smile at Trigger and say something about how it had smelled better when he lived there—but the words caught in her throat when she saw Teddy standing behind him with an evil smirk on his face.

Macie's mouth opened to warn Trigger, but Teddy had already reached out and pressed the prongs of a taser to his side.

The soldier's mouth opened in shock and he fell to the floor with a thump, jerking and moaning.

Chapter Ten

"Trigger!" Macie yelled, then backed up when Teddy calmly stepped over the writhing soldier on the floor.

"You've got something of mine, bitch, and I want it back," Teddy said with deadly intent.

Macie backed up as Teddy kept stalking forward.

"I don't!" she said, feeling the tell-tale signs of a full-blown anxiety attack coursing through her body.

"You do. Where's that stupid box of keepsakes you kept in your closet?" Teddy asked.

Macie blinked in surprise. *That's* where he'd hidden something? She hadn't even looked inside the beaten-up old shoebox because it was the last place she figured anyone would hide anything. It wasn't secure in the slightest, and only held silly, cheap mementoes of her life. Of course, now that she knew that's where Teddy had stashed whatever it was he so desperately wanted, it made sense.

She couldn't come up with an answer fast enough, and he reached forward and wrapped a strong hand around her throat and squeezed.

Macie's hands immediately reached up and tugged at his fingers, to no avail.

She looked into the face, which she had once thought was good-looking, now feeling complete terror. His blue eyes were narrowed in anger and the beard he used to keep trimmed neat was bushy and unkempt. She even saw what looked like food stuck in the hair.

She looked down at the arm she was clawing, still trying to get him to release her, and stared at the tattoo that now adorned it. He hadn't had any tattoos that she'd seen when they'd been dating, but the new ink terrified her. It was a black-and-white design of a naked woman, with her arms tied together in front of her and a knife sticking out of her chest. Blood dripped from the knife, and the words, *Women are like weeds— to be exterminated,* were inked in cursive around the frightening image.

"Where. Is. It?" Teddy bit out, leaning into her and squeezing her neck harder.

Macie's mouth opened and shut, but she couldn't get any words out.

Obviously realizing he was preventing her from speaking, Teddy loosened his grip but didn't let go. "I'll kill you *and* your little friend right here and now if you don't speak up," he threatened.

"Not here," Macie said as soon as she was able. Tricking him didn't even cross her mind.

"You better not be fucking with me," he said.

"I'm not. I took it with me when I left."

"Fucking hell," Teddy swore. "Where is it?"

"Killeen," Macie said. "You can take the keys to the house and go get it. I'll tell you exactly where it is."

"Oh no," Teddy sneered. "You're coming with me. The last thing I want is your fucking boyfriend to walk in on me in his house. You're my ticket to making sure I get what I want and get the hell out of there in one piece."

Macie didn't want to be his ticket to anything. She just wanted him to take his belongings back and get out of her life for good.

Just then, Trigger moaned on the floor next to them, and Teddy swore again.

He raised the taser he still held in his free hand and pressed it to Macie's side. "Nighty-night, bitch," he said, then Macie heard no more as the most intense pain she'd ever felt coursed through her body.

* * * *

Trigger lifted his head and tried to shake off the lethargy he felt. Then he tried to remember where he was and what had happened to him.

Everything was confusing at first—until it all came back at once.

He tried to lurch to his feet, but only got as far as his knees before he had to brace himself on the floor and take a deep breath. "Son of a bitch," he swore, then reached into his pocket for his phone. Thankful it was still there, he swore again when he realized that his keys were missing.

He crawled over to the nearest chair and hauled himself into it before clicking on his commander's number in his contacts.

"Commander Robinson."

"He's got Macie," Trigger said, not prevaricating.

"What? Where are you, Trigger?"

"Lampasas. Macie called me because she knew you were busy and she needed a file from her apartment. I didn't see anything to be concerned about when we got here, but her ex ambushed me from behind. Tased me. Just woke up. She's gone. As are my keys."

"You need an ambulance?" the commander asked, and Trigger shook his head in amazement. The man had just learned his woman had been taken, and yet he was still concerned about *him*. "No, sir. I was incapacitated, but I heard her say something about a box with memorabilia in it."

"That's at my house," the commander said. "Call Lefty. He'll come pick you up. I'm taking the others with me. How long?"

Trigger knew exactly what he meant. He looked at his watch. "I'd estimate between twenty and twenty-five minutes."

"Roger."

And then the phone went silent, and Trigger knew his commander was on the move. He sent up a silent prayer that Macie would be able to keep things together and stay smart until her man could get to her.

Because there was no doubt that Colonel Colton Robinson would get to Macie. And the shape he found her in would determine if Teddy was a dead man or not.

* * * *

Colt clicked off the phone with Oz, one of the Deltas under his command, and knocked on the window of a conference room. He made a hand gesture, and the seven men inside immediately pushed their chairs back and hurried for the door.

Colt didn't bother to wait for them. They caught up and he informed them of what was happening while on the move.

Oz would call the others and have them meet at Colt's house. There wasn't time for them all to gather and come up with a plan. They'd have to wing it.

Within two minutes, Colt was climbing into his Wrangler, and Truck, Ghost, and Fletch had jumped in as well. He was only half-listening as Ghost discussed strategy and who was going to set up a perimeter around the house to make sure Teddy didn't escape once they made entry.

The only thing he could think about was Macie. If one hair on her head was hurt, there'd be hell to pay.

"So he put whatever it was in a box of keepsakes?" Fletch asked.

"I guess. It's a battered old shoebox. Mace told me she kept mementoes of her and Truck in there."

"I'll fucking kill him," Truck said, and Colt knew he needed to get a handle on his men.

"If anyone is killing him, it's *me*. Hear me?"

He heard two "Yes, sirs," and glanced over at Truck.

"Laughlin?"

"No disrespect, sir, but this is my sister."

"And it's the woman I love," Colt retorted. "I need you to keep your head in the game, because *I* can't. I need you to have my back," he told the much larger man. "If I end up in jail, your sister will be alone, and she'll blame herself."

"She won't be alone," Truck countered. "She'll have me and the rest of us."

Colt didn't respond with words, merely glared at his soldier.

Finally, Truck relented. "I understand, sir. And I've got your back. We all do."

Colt nodded. It was as good a plan as they were going to have by the time they turned onto his street. There was no more time to talk.

Trigger's Porsche was sitting in his driveway, and every muscle in Colt's body went on red-alert. They couldn't have been at his house very long, but Macie spending even one minute alone with her asshole ex was too long.

Colt stopped his Jeep two houses down and all four men climbed out without a word. He heard a noise behind him, and turned to see three more cars stop and the rest of his men exit the vehicles. Ghost quickly made contact, and most of the men disappeared into the neighborhood. Colt knew they were taking up positions around his house, making sure Teddy—and, God forbid, anyone else with him—didn't manage to escape.

That left him with Truck and Ghost. Colt looked at his men…and felt an odd calmness settle over his body. Teddy had made the decision to put his hands on Colt's woman and he'd pay the price.

Colt led the way toward his front door. He knew Macie used the security code, and since he hadn't gotten a phone call wanting his passcode, he assumed she'd correctly put in the code when she'd let Teddy inside the house. He very slowly turned the knob on his front door and held his breath as he pushed it open. When the security system didn't immediately start beeping, warning him to put in the code, he thought, *good girl.* Macie hadn't set off the alarm when she'd entered, which would have alerted Colt, but she also hadn't reset it, allowing him and his men to enter undetected.

Colt didn't have a weapon, but he didn't need one. *He* was a weapon. A deadly one.

At first, he didn't hear anyone in the house, and his heart sank with the thought that perhaps he was too late—but then he heard a man's voice coming from upstairs.

Slowly and silently, Colt made his way up the stairs. The farther he went, the clearer he could hear what Teddy was saying.

"You're so stupid! I can't believe you've kept this shit after all these years. What's this? A ticket stub? Fuck…ridiculous. And a napkin? Gross! What's this? A picture? What the fuck *is* this?"

"Don't, Teddy," Macie pleaded, the fear easy to hear in her voice.

"Is this a sonogram? Don't tell me you've got a kid stashed away somewhere?"

"No. *Please*, just give it to me."

"Do you want to know why I picked you?" Teddy asked, but he didn't wait for Macie to reply before he answered his own question. "Because you're *weak*. You're scared of your own shadow. I knew you'd be easy to manipulate, and I was right. But then you had to go and grow a backbone."

"You hid drugs in my apartment," Macie said, her voice shaking.

Colt gestured for Truck and Ghost to pass him and get to the other side of his bedroom door. They needed to make a coordinate entry if they were going to surprise Teddy and get between him and Macie.

"It's not my fault you don't have a shred of human decency in your bones. If you hadn't left me at that restaurant when I had the anxiety attack, I might still be dating you."

"Bitch!" Teddy said.

Then there was the sound of paper tearing, and Macie's anguished voice crying out, "No!"

"Now," Colt whispered—and as a unit, the three soldiers entered the room.

Colt had time to see Macie on her knees on the floor, in front of scattered pieces of paper and other odds and ends.

Theodore Dorentes saw them before Macie did, and he lunged for her with the taser he held in his hand.

Later, Colt mused that perhaps he would've reacted differently if the man had come after *him* with the taser...but he didn't. He targeted Macie, who wasn't even looking at him and couldn't protect herself.

Colt threw himself at Teddy. The prongs of the taser cracked in the oddly quiet room, but Colt didn't even feel them touch his chest. His arm was already moving toward the other man's face and even though the electricity moving through Colt's system jammed up his nerves, he threw his body weight behind his fist and managed to crash into Teddy with his body as he fell.

He felt Teddy's nose break under his fist, and his head snapped back with the power of the punch.

Both men landed in a heap just feet from Macie. In seconds, Ghost was pulling Teddy out from under Colt and kicking the taser away. Colt forced his body to move, thankful that, once his fist had hit Teddy's face, the man had dropped the device.

By the time Colt had regained his senses and turned to Macie, Truck had already wrapped her in his arms and turned his back, protecting his sister from whatever might happen next.

Colt crawled to the siblings and jerked at Truck's arm. Surprisingly, Truck let go of his sister and all but thrust her into Colt's arms. He felt Macie trembling, and assumed the same position Truck had, holding her in his arms and protecting her by turning his back to the room.

Within moments, the room was full of several pissed-off, amped-up Special Forces soldiers, but all Colt could do was bury his face in Macie's hair and rock back and forth.

Eventually, he realized that instead of being hysterical, she was trying to calm *him*.

"I'm okay, Colt. You got here in time. I'm okay."

Taking a deep breath, Colt picked his head up and realized that he'd been crying, and he hadn't even noticed. Macie shifted in his embrace and wiped the tears from his cheeks. "I'm fine," she whispered.

"He's dead," Ghost said matter-of-factly.

"Dead?" Macie gasped.

It was the tone of her voice that snapped Colt out of the daze he'd been in. He stood and helped Macie to her feet as well. Then he pressed her cheek to his chest and turned to look at Teddy and Ghost.

The man was lying on the floor, his eyes open and staring unseeingly up at the ceiling.

"If I had to guess, I'd say you severed an artery in his brain. The force of his head twisting probably broke the artery, then him hitting the ground didn't help any. He's definitely dead," Ghost confirmed.

"Fuck," Colt said under his breath. He hadn't meant to kill the man, just to keep him from hurting Macie.

"Self-defense," Lucky said definitively.

Colt turned to look at him. "It was, but I'm not sure anyone will believe me."

"They will when they see the video," Lucky said nonchalantly.

"Video?" Macie asked, her voice muffled from being pressed against Colt's chest.

"Never leave home without it," Lucky quipped. "Grabbed your ladder and was going to breach the window after you made your move. I caught it all on video. Commander, you were definitely protecting Macie from being further harmed."

Colt closed his eyes in relief.

He felt a hand on his shoulder and turned to look at Truck. "Owe you, sir. Huge."

Colt eyed the large man and pressed his luck while he could. "I want permission to ask your sister to marry me. Since her dad is an asshole, I've got no one to ask but you."

He heard Macie gasp and felt her tighten her arms around him, but Colt kept his gaze on Truck's.

The two men eyed each other for a long moment before Truck

nodded. "One condition."

"Name it," Colt said.

"I want to be there to give her away. Don't care if you do a courthouse quickie, fly to Vegas, or have the full-blown shindig. I want to be there."

"Deal," Colt said without having to think about it. It wasn't even a concession, he'd already planned to ask Truck to be at their wedding, wherever and whenever it happened.

"Ma'am?" Grover said in his deep, rumbly voice.

Colt turned to see his soldier holding pieces of paper that had been torn.

Macie gasped and reached for it with a cry. She held the sonogram of her long-lost baby in her hands and sobbed.

Colt felt helpless. He didn't know what to do to make this better.

"Can I see it?" Brain asked.

Macie let the other man take the pieces from her.

"I think I can fix this," Brain said, once he'd examined the sonogram.

Colt glared at him, not wanting him to get Macie's hopes up.

"You can?" she asked.

"Well, I can't make it perfect, but I can scan the pieces and put them back together on the computer and reprint it. It won't be like new, but it'll be pretty darn close," Brain said with confidence.

Colt could see Truck looking on with the saddest expression on his face as he realized what Brain was holding, and why his sister was so upset. It was obvious brother and sister needed to talk.

"I'd appreciate that," Macie said, her voice breaking.

"I've called the police," Ghost said, interrupting the moment. "I would advise that everyone but Truck, Macie, myself, the commander, and Lucky disappear. Lucky, we need you to stay since you have the video. Leave everything where it is. Evidence."

Colt knew he should be taking control instead of Ghost but the only person he was concerned about at the moment was Macie. He picked her up and carried her out of the room and headed downstairs to await the cops.

* * * *

Two hours later, Macie felt as if her head was going to explode. She was sitting on Colt's lap on the couch, with his arms around her. Truck had gotten her a Vistaril tablet, but it hadn't helped the anxiety migraine that had begun the moment she'd woken up in Trigger's Porsche with Teddy driving.

She'd explained to the police at least three times everything she remembered. Teddy had bragged he'd killed the two thugs who'd broken into her apartment because they'd failed in their attempts at recovering her keepsake box. That was why the cops hadn't been able to find them.

Then she'd learned he'd stashed a small amount of drugs in her box, but that wasn't why he was so desperate to get his hands on it again. He'd also put a list of his suppliers in there. He knew if she found it and gave it to the cops, he was a dead man. His suppliers would kill him for being so careless. For someone as desperate as he was, he was also scarily patient. He'd waited weeks for Macie to show back up at her apartment so he could confront her himself and find out what she'd done with the shoebox. It was fairly obvious that he'd planned on killing her, just like he had his "friends," after he got the list back.

Macie was glad to find out Trigger was all right. Apparently, Teddy had beaten him after tasing him a second time, to try to ensure he was knocked out for a long while, giving Teddy time to get to Killeen and collect his list.

She made sure the officers interviewing her knew she believed Teddy when he'd said he was going to kill her. Colt had reassured her before the cops got there that he wouldn't be arrested. The "stand your ground" law that the state of Texas had meant that he didn't need to attempt to retreat on his own property before using deadly force to defend himself or Macie. Colt really had saved her life. Macie had no doubt about that and she also had no doubt Teddy would've tortured her before he'd killed her if he had the chance.

Thanks to Lucky, who apparently always seemed to be in the right place at the right time, and his video, the cops didn't arrest Colt. After checking his background and finding out what he did on the Army post, they'd warned him not to leave town and to be available for any questions they might have, but they didn't handcuff him and bring him to the station to be questioned.

Macie kept her eyes averted when the coroner came and wheeled Teddy's body out of the house. The entire situation seemed surreal to her.

Truck, Ghost, and Lucky had stayed the entire time the police questioned her and Colt. At one point, Truck disappeared upstairs and came back down with her shoebox. He carefully placed it next to her laptop on the dining room table and gave her a look, which Macie knew meant he would want to talk about its contents later.

Looking at her laptop, Macie winced.

"What is it? Are you in pain?" Colt asked.

"No. I mean, yes, but it's not that," Macie said. "I went to my apartment to get a file I needed to help an author with her website, but I never did get it, and she still needs help."

"I'm sure she'll understand," Truck said.

"No. She won't. You don't get it. These authors rely on me to get their work done. Yeah, she might feel bad about what happened, but that doesn't mean she still doesn't need her websites fixed."

"You can do it tomorrow," Colt said softly. "I'll have one of the guys go to your apartment and pack up all your stuff and bring it here. Then you won't have to worry what you have and don't have anymore."

Even though her head hurt, and she wanted nothing more to sit in a dark room and sleep, Macie turned to Colt. "Did you just ask me to move in with you?"

"No," he said. "I *told* you that you're moving in with me."

Macie snorted and closed her eyes. She put her head on his shoulder and sighed. "I'm too tired and my head hurts too much to argue with you right now."

She heard rustling, and she heard Truck and Lefty say their goodbyes to Colt. Then the room was silent, and still Macie didn't open her eyes.

"If you truly don't want to move in, I'm willing to compromise," Colt told her softly.

Finally feeling mellow because of the pill she'd taken, Macie said, "There's nothing I want more than to move in with you, Colt. I just can't help but wonder what everyone else will think. We haven't known each other that long."

"I don't care," Colt said after a moment. "And I don't care what anyone else thinks. I only care about what *you* think. If you honestly think it's too fast, then I'll back off and we can have sleepovers at each other's places. I want you to be comfortable with our relationship. But

I'll tell you where I stand—I've already been looking at rings. I've asked your brother for permission to ask you to marry me. I've warned my superior officer that I might need some time off in the near future so I can go on my honeymoon…and I've been asking around to learn who's the best OBGYN in the area. I'm in this for the long haul, hon. I can't replace the daughter you lost, but I can do whatever it takes to give you more children."

"You want kids?" she asked incredulously.

"Honestly? I didn't before I met you. But now I can't stop thinking about what an amazing mother you'll be. I can almost picture your beautiful eyes and features on our children. If you don't mind me being an old fart by the time they get into high school, then I'm willing to give you as many children as you want."

Macie could feel her heart beating fast in her chest, but for once today it wasn't because of her anxiety. Oh, she was still nervous as hell about moving in with Colt, but she couldn't help but be excited about the prospect of spending the rest of her life with him.

"If you get thrown in prison will I get conjugal visits?" she teased.

Colt rolled his eyes. "Thanks to Lucky, I'm not going to prison. Are you… I didn't mean to kill him," Colt said, and Macie could hear the uneasiness in his tone. She hated that he was unsure about her reaction to what he'd done.

Forcing her eyes open, she sat up and straddled the man she loved. She stared him in the eyes and said clearly, "I know you didn't. And you did what you had to do. I feel safer with every day that passes because of you. I know that you'll be the most protective dad any kid could ever have, and that eases my mind."

He sighed in relief.

"But I'm always going to be a nervous wreck," Macie warned him. "And if we have kids, it'll probably get worse. I'm going to need you to balance that out with our children. The last thing I want is for them to learn to be afraid of the world like I am."

"You're not afraid of the world," Colt countered. "And I love you exactly the way you are. You make me feel needed. Sure, I could go out and find a woman who was sure of herself one hundred percent of the time and who could take care of herself and all fourteen of her kids, but that's not what I want. That's not *who* I want. I want you. Every gorgeous, beautiful inch of you. You're not flawed in my eyes, Macie.

You're perfect, and I'll remind you every day of our lives if you [..]t me."

"I'd love to move in with you," Macie told him quietly.

"Good. I'll call my men in the morning, and your stuff wi[..] be here by noon, and you can fix your author's website, and we can b[..] back in bed trying to make a baby by dinner time."

Macie rolled her eyes and chuckled. He was pushing his [..]ck, but she didn't call him on it. "I'm ready for a nap," she said instead.

Without a word, Colt stood, taking Macie with him. She [..]rapped her legs around his waist and felt his hands under her ass, holdi[..]g her to him as he walked toward the stairs. He took her to the guest [..]om and laid her on the queen-size bed.

When she started to ask, he put his finger over her lips. [..]Just for tonight. Tomorrow is soon enough to face any lingering demo[..]s in that room. Okay?"

"Okay," she said. Then, as an afterthought, she asked, "[..] there a way out of this room...just in case?"

He smiled down at her and brushed her hair off her fore[..]ead and nodded toward the window. "I went out and bought rope lad[..]ers after you jumped out of your apartment window. There's one in ev[..]ry room on this floor."

"I love you," Macie said as she shut her eyes.

She felt Colt's lips on her forehead and heard him say, "I [..]ve you, too."

Epilogue

"Can I ask you something?" Macie said.

Colt chuckled and tightened his arm around his wife's waist. They were lying naked and replete in each others' arms. They were on their honeymoon in a fancy resort in the Caribbean. It had cost an arm and a leg to rent the room right on the water, but it had been worth every penny when he'd seen how relieved Macie had been.

At six months pregnant, he thought she was the most beautiful woman alive, but she wasn't quite ready to parade around the public beaches with her baby belly.

"I keep telling you that you don't ever have to ask me if it's okay to ask me anything. You can just ask," Colt told her, grinning.

She twirled her finger around one of his nipples, and Colt forced himself to pay attention to what she was saying instead of throwing her on her back and fucking her again.

Macie had gotten pregnant almost as soon as they'd begun trying. She'd been knocked up so quickly, he hadn't even officially asked her to marry him. He'd rectified that immediately, and the same night she'd said yes, he'd called Truck and told him to clear his schedule because as soon as they could get an appointment, they were getting married by a justice of the peace.

Colt knew without asking that Macie would hate a big wedding. She'd hate to have all those people staring at her and she'd worry herself to death over every little detail. So the small ceremony at the courthouse suited him just fine.

That didn't prevent the wives of the men under his command from throwing them a big-ass party. Colt had been relieved that Macie didn't seem to mind, and in fact had the time of her life that night.

"Mary told me about that one mission you went on, and you explained what happened…but I heard her talking with Casey later and she said something else about you."

Colt didn't even tense at the reminder of that day so long ago. Macie didn't love him any less as a result, and he'd finally come to terms with it himself. Gris and his family had shown up at their wedding party as a surprise. Truck had found out about the man and had called to invite him. It was so good to see his friend so happy and settled, it helped with any remaining guilt Colt felt about what had happened all those years ago.

"What'd she say, hon?" Colt asked.

"She was asking Casey if she should tell me about a time when you refused to allow one of the soldiers in your unit to leave when his baby was born."

Colt knew exactly what she was talking about. "Mary's right. I *did* do that."

"Why?"

Colt smiled. He loved that Macie didn't get huffy with him or tell him he was coldhearted. She always gave people the benefit of the doubt. It was one of the million and two things he loved about her.

"The soldier in question was married at the time, and the woman having his baby wasn't his wife. He had been cheating on his wife for months. My hands were tied. Under the Uniform Code of Military Justice, adultery is unacceptable conduct and a soldier can be demoted as a result. This guy wasn't legally separated, and he didn't give a shit who knew about this other woman. Not only that, but the other woman knew he was married, and apparently *she* didn't care either.

"I refused to let the soldier take leave because I knew he was going to lie to his wife about where he was going and why. Not only did I not let him go, I did my best to push for a court-martial as well."

"Wow. Did he get kicked out of the Army?" Macie asked, coming up on an elbow so she could look at his face.

Colt shook his head. "No. He was demoted to private, but he was allowed to stay. Those are the kinds of soldier I hate. They aren't in the armed forces to serve their country. I don't mind the men and women who join for college money, or because they need to support their family, or even because they have no idea what to do with their lives. But I hate the ones who're trying to milk every penny they can out of the government. They're often cowards or bullies, and are part of the reason why I jumped at the chance to command the Delta Force units here in Texas."

Macie put her head back down on his shoulder.

"Any more questions?"

She shook her head. "No. And for the record, I knew you had to have a good reason. It's just not in you to be an ass for the sake of being an ass."

Colt chuckled. "I can definitely be an ass," he told her. "Just ask your brother."

Macie shook her head. "No. That's different. You were doing so to help them become better soldiers."

"He told you stories then, huh?" Colt asked.

He felt Macie smile against him.

"Yeah. I heard some stuff," she agreed.

"You and Truck are good, right?"

Macie nodded. "Yeah. It was tough to talk to him, but I told him all about my baby and what our parents did. He was pissed, like you were, but he didn't judge me like I thought he would. It's good to have him back in my life," she admitted.

"I know he feels the same way," Colt reassured her.

They didn't say anything for a while, just listened to the sound of the waves on the beach outside the screen door of their room.

"I'm worried about Trigger and the others," she eventually said.

"Why?"

"Because they're lonely."

"What? Why do you think that?"

"I can just tell," Macie said.

"I'm sure when the time is right, the right woman will come along for each of them," Colt reassured his wife.

"But what if they're not looking for her? She could be right under their noses and they wouldn't even know it. They'd overlook her, then possibly be lonely for the rest of their lives."

Colt held back the chuckle that threatened. The hormones coursing through Macie's body were making her extra emotional about everything lately. He loved that she was worried about his men, but knew they'd laugh their asses off if they heard her assessment of their love lives. "They'll know her when they see her," he told her.

"Hmmm," she mumbled, obviously not convinced.

Making a mental note to warn Trigger that his wife was on a mission to see him and the rest of the men on his team happy settled down, Colt decided to get her attention off of them and back on him.

He shifted until he was braced over Macie and kissed his way down her body. He spent a lot of time kissing and caressing her beautiful baby belly, and muttering words of love to their daughter nestled within, then continued until he was between her legs.

"Again?" she mock complained.

"Again," Colt confirmed as he lowered his head. He knew Macie loved this, almost more than any other way he made love to her, and he was determined to make sure she *loved* every second of their honeymoon.

He'd do anything for his wife. Move heaven and Earth to make her happy and content. He might've saved her from her ex, but she'd more than paid that back to him tenfold. He was happier than he'd ever been in his life and had never looked forward to the future more than he did now.

Life was good. He held the proof in his hands.

* * * *

Trigger and the rest of his team *will* get their happy-ever-after starting next year. Stay tuned for a new Delta Force Heroes series featuring the same kind of protective alpha men and strong women you've come to know and love.

In the meantime, if you haven't read about Truck and his team, you can start the series right now for free with *Rescuing Rayne*!

* * * *

Hopefully after reading Colt and Macie's story you'll want to read more about Truck, the commander, and the rest of the Delta Force team mentioned in the book. Be sure to download Rescuing Rayne. It's the first book in the Delta Force Heroes Series and is FREE on all platforms!

As a flight attendant, Rayne Jackson is used to cancellations, but she never dreamed her latest would lead to a whirlwind tour of London with a handsome stranger...or a life-altering night in his bed. One evening is all the enigmatic man can give her, and Rayne greedily takes it, despite suspecting it will never be enough.

Heading home after another extreme mission, Keane "Ghost" Bryson hadn't planned to seduce someone during his layover, but Rayne is too sweet to resist. Being a Delta Force member means lying to protect his identity, which is unfortunate, considering Rayne seems made for Ghost, right down to the tattoo on her back. For the first time in his life, regret fills him as he slips away the following morning.

Both are shocked when, months later, they meet again—under the worst possible circumstances. Seems fate has given them a second chance...if they can survive the terrorist situation they're in. If Rayne can forgive Ghost his lies. And if Ghost can trust Rayne to be strong enough to endure the secrets and uncertainty that come with loving a Delta Force soldier.

* * * *

And if you enjoyed Rescuing Macie, you'll like *all* my books because I write much the same way in each of my series. Check out the first book in my new SEAL of Protection: Legacy Series, Securing Caite.

Caite McCallan is a Department of Defense admin working in Bahrain when a glitchy elevator, of all things, leads to an unexpected invitation to dinner by a gorgeous Navy SEAL. When he later stands her up, Caite's understandably upset...until she overhears a plot that confirms Rocco didn't blow her off. Instead, he and two fellow SEALs are in danger—and Caite is forced to put her career and her life on the line to save them.

Blake "Rocco" Wise never expected his routine mission to go

sideways, but he was even more surprised to find himself and his teammates rescued by the adorably shy woman he met in ι stalled elevator. Caite's selfless act saved his life, but when attempts or her own make it clear someone wants her gone, it's Rocco's turn to pι ιtect the brave, sweet, sexy woman. The longer he knows her, the more ιe wants her...but keeping Caite close could bring her nearer to the en my than ever before.

* * * *

Also from 1001 Dark Nights and Susan Stoker, discover Rescui g Sadie.

Discover 1001 Dark Nights Collection 8

QUIET MAN by Kristen Ashley
A Dream Man Novella

ABANDON by Rachel Van Dyken
A Seaside Pictures Novella

THE OPEN DOOR by Laurelin Paige
A Found Duet Novella

CLOSER by Kylie Scott
A Stage Dive Novella

SOMETHING JUST LIKE THIS by Jennifer Probst
A Stay Novella

BLOOD NIGHT by Heather Graham
A Krewe of Hunters Novella

TWIST OF FATE by Jill Shalvis
A Heartbreaker Bay Novella

MORE THAN PLEASURE YOU by Shayla Black
A More Than Words Novella

WONDER WITH ME by Kristen Proby
A With Me In Seattle Novella

THE DARKEST ASSASSIN by Gena Showalter
A Lords of the Underworld Novella

Also from 1001 Dark Nights:
DAMIEN by J. Kenner
A Stark Novel

Discover 1001 Dark Nights

COLLECTION THREE
HIDDEN INK by Carrie Ann Ryan
BLOOD ON THE BAYOU by Heather Graham
SEARCHING FOR MINE by Jennifer Probst
DANCE OF DESIRE by Christopher Rice
ROUGH RHYTHM by Tessa Bailey
DEVOTED by Lexi Blake
Z by Larissa Ione
FALLING UNDER YOU by Laurelin Paige
EASY FOR KEEPS by Kristen Proby
UNCHAINED by Elisabeth Naughton
HARD TO SERVE by Laura Kaye
DRAGON FEVER by Donna Grant
KAYDEN/SIMON by Alexandra Ivy/Laura Wright
STRUNG UP by Lorelei James
MIDNIGHT UNTAMED by Lara Adrian
TRICKED by Rebecca Zanetti
DIRTY WICKED by Shayla Black
THE ONLY ONE by Lauren Blakely
SWEET SURRENDER by Liliana Hart

COLLECTION FOUR
ROCK CHICK REAWAKENING by Kristen Ashley
ADORING INK by Carrie Ann Ryan
SWEET RIVALRY by K. Bromberg
SHADE'S LADY by Joanna Wylde
RAZR by Larissa Ione
ARRANGED by Lexi Blake
TANGLED by Rebecca Zanetti
HOLD ME by J. Kenner
SOMEHOW, SOME WAY by Jennifer Probst
TOO CLOSE TO CALL by Tessa Bailey
HUNTED by Elisabeth Naughton
EYES ON YOU by Laura Kaye
BLADE by Alexandra Ivy/Laura Wright
DRAGON BURN by Donna Grant
TRIPPED OUT by Lorelei James
STUD FINDER by Lauren Blakely

MIDNIGHT UNLEASHED by Lara Adrian
HALLOW BE THE HAUNT by Heather Graham
DIRTY FILTHY FIX by Laurelin Paige
THE BED MATE by Kendall Ryan
NIGHT GAMES by CD Reiss
NO RESERVATIONS by Kristen Proby
DAWN OF SURRENDER by Liliana Hart

COLLECTION FIVE
BLAZE ERUPTING by Rebecca Zanetti
ROUGH RIDE by Kristen Ashley
HAWKYN by Larissa Ione
RIDE DIRTY by Laura Kaye
ROME'S CHANCE by Joanna Wylde
THE MARRIAGE ARRANGEMENT by Jennifer Probst
SURRENDER by Elisabeth Naughton
INKED NIGHTS by Carrie Ann Ryan
ENVY by Rachel Van Dyken
PROTECTED by Lexi Blake
THE PRINCE by Jennifer L. Armentrout
PLEASE ME by J. Kenner
WOUND TIGHT by Lorelei James
STRONG by Kylie Scott
DRAGON NIGHT by Donna Grant
TEMPTING BROOKE by Kristen Proby
HAUNTED BE THE HOLIDAYS by Heather Graham
CONTROL by K. Bromberg
HUNKY HEARTBREAKER by Kendall Ryan
THE DARKEST CAPTIVE by Gena Showalter

Also from 1001 Dark Nights:

TAME ME by J. Kenner
THE SURRENDER GATE By Christopher Rice
SERVICING THE TARGET By Cherise Sinclair
TEMPT ME by J. Kenner

About Susan Stoker

New York Times, USA Today, #1 Amazon Bestseller, and Wall Street Journal Bestselling Author, Susan Stoker has a heart as big as the state of Tennessee where she lives, but this all American girl has also spent the last eighteen years living in Missouri, California, Colorado, Indiana, and Texas. She's married to a retired Army man (and current firefighter/EMT) who now gets to follow her around the country.

She debuted her first series in 2014 and quickly followed that up with the SEAL of Protection Series, which solidified her love of writing and creating stories readers can get lost in.

Connect with her at www.StokerAces.com

Discover More Susan Stoker

Rescuing Sadie: A Delta Force Heroes/Masters and Mercenaries Novella by Susan Stoker

Sadie Jennings was used to being protected. As the niece of Sean Taggart, and the receptionist at McKay-Taggart Group, she was constantly surrounded by Alpha men more than capable, and willing, to lay down their life for her. But when she visits her friend in San Antonio, and acts on suspicious activity at Milena's workplace, Sadie puts both of them in the crosshairs of a madman. After several harrowing weeks, her friend is now safe, but for Sadie, the repercussions of her rash act linger on.

Chase Jackson, no stranger to dangerous situations as a captain in the US Army, has volunteered himself as Sadie's bodyguard. He fell head over heels for the beautiful woman the first time he laid eyes on her. With a Delta Force team at his back, he reassures the Taggart's that Sadie will be safe. But when the situation in San Antonio catches up with her, Chase has to use everything he's learned over his career to keep his promise...and to keep Sadie alive long enough to officially make her his.

On behalf of 1001 Dark Nights,

Liz Berry and M.J. Rose would like to thank ~

Steve Berry
Doug Scofield
Kim Guidroz
Jillian Stein
InkSlinger PR
Dan Slater
Asha Hossain
Chris Graham
Fedora Chen
Kasi Alexander
Jessica Johns
Dylan Stockton
Richard Blake
and Simon Lipskar

43056142R00083

Made in the USA
Middletown, DE
19 April 2019